I0567230

W.W. JACOBS – THE SHORT STORIES
VOLUME 10

William Wymark Jacobs was born on September 8th, 1863 in the Wapping district of London, England. Jacobs grew up near the docks, where his father was a wharf manager. The docks and river side would be a constant theme of his writing in years to come.

Although surrounded by poverty, he received a formal education in London, first at a private prep school and later at the Birkbeck Literary and Scientific Institute.

His working life began with a less than exciting clerical position at the Post Office Savings Bank. Jacobs put his imagination to good use writing short stories, sketches and articles, many for the Post Office house publication "Blackfriars Magazine."

In 1896 Jacobs published Many Cargoes, a selection of sea-faring yarns, which established him as a popular writer with a knack for authentic dialogue and trick endings.

A year later he published a novelette, The Skipper's Wooing, and in 1898 another collection of short stories; Sea Urchins. These works painted vivid pictures of dockland and seafaring London full of colourful characters.

By 1899, Jacobs was able to quit the post office and write full-time.

He married the noted suffragist Agnes Eleanor Williams (who had been jailed for her protest activities) in 1900. They set up households both in Loughton, Essex and in central London.

The publication in 1902 of At Sunwich Port and Dialstone Lane, in 1904, cemented Jacobs' reputation as one of the leading British authors of the new century.

There followed a string of further successful publications, including Captain's All (1905), Night Watches (1914), The Castaways (1916), and Sea Whispers (1926).

Though Jacobs would create little in the way of new work after 1911, he still wrote and was recognized as a leading humorist, ranked alongside such writers as P. G. Wodehouse.

William Wymark Jacobs died in a North London nursing home in Hornsey Lane, Islington on September 1st, 1943.

Index of Contents

THE TEMPTATION OF SAMUEL BURGE

Mr. Higgs, jeweller, sat in the small parlour behind his shop, gazing hungrily at a supper-table which had been laid some time before. It was a quarter to ten by the small town clock on the mantelpiece, and the jeweller rubbing his hands over the fire tried in vain to remember what etiquette had to say about starting a meal before the arrival of an expected guest.

"He must be coming by the last train after all, sir," said the housekeeper entering the room and glancing at the clock. "I suppose these London gentlemen keep such late hours they don't understand us country folk wanting to get to bed in decent time. You must be wanting your supper, sir."

Mr. Higgs sighed. "I shall be glad of my supper," he said slowly, "but I dare say our friend is hungrier still. Travelling is hungry work."

"Perhaps he is thinking over his words for the seventh day," said the housekeeper solemnly. "Forgetting hunger and thirst and all our poor earthly feelings in the blessedness of his work."

"Perhaps so," assented the other, whose own earthly feelings were particularly strong just at that moment.

"Brother Simpson used to forget all about meal-times when he stayed here," said the housekeeper, clasping her hands. "He used to sit by the window with his eyes half-closed and shake his head at the smell from the kitchen and call it flesh-pots of Egypt. He said that if it wasn't for keeping up his strength for the work, luscious bread and fair water was all he wanted. I expect Brother Burge will be a similar sort of man."

"Brother Clark wrote and told me that he only lives for the work," said the jeweller, with another glance at the clock. "The chapel at Clerkenwell is crowded to hear him. It's a blessed favour and privilege to have such a selected instrument staying in the house. I'm curious to see him; from what Brother Clark said I rather fancy that he was a little bit wild in his younger days."

"Hallelujah!" exclaimed the housekeeper with fervour. "I mean to think as he's seen the error of his ways," she added sharply, as her master looked up.

"There he is," said the latter, as the bell rang.

The housekeeper went to the side-door, and drawing back the bolt admitted the gentleman whose preaching had done so much for the small but select sect known as the Seventh Day Primitive Apostles. She came back into the room followed by a tall stout man, whose upper lip and short stubby beard streaked with grey seemed a poor match for the beady eyes which lurked behind a pair of clumsy spectacles.

"Brother Samuel Burge?" inquired the jeweller, rising.

The visitor nodded, and regarding him with a smile charged with fraternal love, took his hand in a huge grip and shook it fervently.

"I am glad to see you, Brother Higgs," he said, regarding him fondly. "Oh, 'ow my eyes have yearned to be set upon you! Oh, 'ow my ears 'ave longed to hearken unto the words of your voice!"

He breathed thickly, and taking a seat sat with his hands upon his knees, looking at a fine piece of cold beef which the housekeeper had just placed upon the table.

"Is Brother Clark well?" inquired the jeweller, placing a chair for him at the table and taking up his carving-knife.

"Dear Brother Clark is in excellent 'ealth, I thank you," said the other, taking the proffered chair. "Oh! what a man he is; what a instrument for good. Always stretching out them blessed hands of 'is to make one of the fallen a Seventh Day Primitive."

"And success attends his efforts?" said the jeweller.

"Success, Brother!" repeated Mr. Burge, eating rapidly and gesticulating with his knife. "Success ain't no name for it. Why, since this day last week he has saved three pick-pockets, two Salvationists, one bigamist and a Roman Catholic."

Brother Higgs murmured his admiration. "You are also a power for good," he said wistfully. "Brother Clark tells me in his letter that your exhortations have been abundantly blessed."

Mr. Burge shook his head. "A lot of it falls by the wayside," he said modestly, "but some of it is an eye-opener to them as don't entirely shut their ears. Only the day before yesterday I 'ad two jemmies and a dark lantern sent me with a letter saying as 'ow the owner had no further use for 'em."

The jeweller's eyes glistened with admiration not quite untinged with envy. "Have you expounded the Word for long?" he inquired.

"Six months," replied the other. "It come to me quite natural—I was on the penitent bench on the Saturday, and the Wednesday afterwards I preached as good a sermon as ever I've preached in my life. Brother Clark said it took 'is breath away."

"And he's a judge too," said the admiring jeweller.

"Now," continued Brother Burge, helping himself plentifully to pickled walnuts. "Now there ain't standing room in our Bethel when I'm expounding. People come to hear me from all parts—old and young—rich and poor—and the Apostles that don't come early 'ave to stand outside and catch the crumbs I throw 'em through the winders."

"It is enough," sighed Brother Higgs, whose own audience was frequently content to be on the wrong side of the window, "it is enough to make a man vain."

"I struggle against it, Brother," said Mr. Burge, passing his cup up for some more tea. "I fight against it hard, but once the Evil One was almost too much for me; and in spite of myself, and knowing besides that it was a plot of 'is, I nearly felt uplifted."

Brother Higgs, passing him some more beef, pressed for details.

"He sent me two policemen," replied the other, scowling darkly at the meanness of the trick. "One I might 'ave stood, but two come to being pretty near too much for me. They sat under me while I gave 'em the Word 'ot and strong, and the feeling I had standing up there and telling policemen what they ought to do I shall never forget."

"But why should policemen make you proud?" asked his puzzled listener.

Mr. Burge looked puzzled in his turn. "Why, hasn't Brother Clark told you about me?" he inquired.

Mr. Higgs shook his head. "He sort of—suggested that—that you had been a little bit wild before you came to us," he murmured apologetically.

"A—little—bit—wild?" repeated Brother Burge, in horrified accents. "ME? a little bit wild?"

"No doubt he exaggerated a little," said the jeweller hurriedly. "Being such a good man himself, no doubt things would seem wild to him that wouldn't to us—to me, I mean."

"A little bit wild," said his visitor again. "Sam Burge, the Converted Burglar, a little bit wild. Well, well!"

"Converted what?" shouted the jeweller, half-rising from his chair.

"Burglar," said the other shortly. "Why, I should think I know more about the inside o' gaols than anybody in England; I've pretty near killed three policemen, besides breaking a gent's leg and throwing a footman out of window, and then Brother Clark goes and says I've been a little bit wild. I wonder what he would 'ave?"

"But you—you've quite reformed now?" said the jeweller, resuming his seat and making a great effort to hide his consternation.

"I 'ope so," said Mr. Burge, with alarming humility; "but it's an uncertain world, and far be it from me to boast. That's why I've come here."

Mr. Higgs, only half-comprehending, sat back gasping.

"If I can stand this," pursued Brother Burge, gesticulating wildly in the direction of the shop, "if I can stand being here with all these 'ere pretty little things to be 'ad for the trouble of picking of 'em up, I can stand anything. Tempt me, I says to Brother Clark. Put me in the way o' temptation, I says. Let me see whether the Evil One or me is the strongest; let me 'ave a good old up and down with the Powers o' Darkness, and see who wins."

Mr. Higgs, gripping the edge of the table with both hands, gazed at this new Michael in speechless consternation.

"I think I see his face now," said Brother Burge, with tender enthusiasm. "All in a glow it was, and he patted me on the shoulder and says, 'I'll send you on a week's mission to Duncombe,' he says, and 'you shall stop with Brother Higgs who 'as a shop full o' cunning wrought vanities in silver and gold.'"

"But suppose," said the jeweller, finding his voice by a great effort, "suppose victory is not given unto you."

"It won't make any difference," replied his visitor. "Brother Clark promised that it shouldn't. 'If you fall, Brother,' he says, 'we'll help you up again. When you are tired of sin come back to us—there's always a welcome.'"

"But—" began the dismayed jeweller.

"We can only do our best," said Brother Burge, "the rest we must leave. I 'ave girded my loins for the fray, and taken much spiritual sustenance on the way down from this little hymn-book."

Mr. Higgs paid no heed. He sat marvelling over the fatuousness of Brother Clark and trying to think of ways and means out of the dilemma into which that gentleman's perverted enthusiasm had placed him. He wondered whether it would be possible to induce Brother Burge to sleep elsewhere by offering to bear his hotel expenses, and at last, after some hesitation, broached the subject.

"What!" exclaimed the other, pushing his plate from him and regarding him with great severity. "Go and sleep at a hotel? After Brother Clark has been and took all this trouble? Why, I wouldn't think of doing such a thing."

"Brother Clark has no right to expose you to such a trial," said Mr. Higgs with great warmth.

"I wonder what he'd say if he 'eard you," remarked Mr. Burge sternly. "After his going and making all these arrangements, for you to try and go and upset 'em. To ask me to shun the fight like a coward; to ask me to go and hide in the rear-ranks in a hotel with everything locked up, or a Coffer Pallis with nothing to steal."

"I should sleep far more comfortably if I knew that you were not undergoing this tremendous strain,' said the unhappy Mr. Higgs, "and besides that, if you did give way, it would be a serious business for me —that's what I want you to look at. I am afraid that if—if unhappily you did fall, I couldn't prevent you."

"I'm sure you couldn't," said the other cordially. "That's the beauty of it; that's when the Evil One's whispers get louder and louder. Why, I could choke you between my finger and thumb. If unfortunately my fallen nature should be too strong for me, don't interfere whatever you do. I mightn't be myself."

Mr. Higgs rose and faced him gasping.

"Not even—call for—the police—I suppose," he jerked out.

"That would be interfering," said Brother Burge coldly.

The jeweller tried to think. It was past eleven. The housekeeper had gone to spend the night with an ailing sister, and a furtive glance at Brother Burge's small shifty eyes and fat unwholesome face was sufficient to deter him from leaving him alone with his property, while he went to ask the police to give an eye to his house for the night. Besides, it was more than probable that Mr. Burge would decline to allow such a proceeding. With a growing sense of his peril he resolved to try flattery.

"It was a great thing for the Brethren to secure a man like you," he said.

"I never thought they'd ha' done it," said Mr. Burge frankly. "I've 'ad all sorts trying to convert me; crying over me and praying over me. I remember the first dear good man that called me a lorst lamb. He didn't say anything else for a month."

"So upset," hazarded the jeweller.

"I broke his jor, pore feller," said Brother Burge, a sad but withal indulgent smile lighting up his face at the vagaries of his former career. "What time do you go to bed, Brother?"

"Any time," said the other reluctantly. "I suppose you are tired with your journey?"

Mr. Burge assented, and rising from his chair yawned loudly and stretched himself. In the small room with his huge arms raised he looked colossal.

"I suppose," said the jeweller, still seeking to re-assure himself, "I suppose dear Brother Clark felt pretty certain of you, else he wouldn't have sent you here?"

"Brother Clark said 'What is a jeweller's shop compared with a 'uman soul, a priceless 'uman soul?'" replied Mr. Burge. "What is a few gew-gaws to decorate them that perish, and make them vain, when you come to consider the opportunity of such a trial, and the good it'll do and the draw it'll be—if I do win—and testify to the congregation to that effect? Why, there's sermons for a lifetime in it."

"So there is," said the jeweller, trying to look cheerful. "You've got a good face, Brother Burge, and you'll do a lot of good by your preaching. There is honesty written in every feature."

Mr. Burge turned and surveyed himself in the small pier-glass. "Yes," he said, somewhat discontentedly, "I don't look enough like a burglar to suit some of 'em."

"Some people are hard to please," said the other warmly.

Mr. Burge started and eyed him thoughtfully, and then as Mr. Higgs after some hesitation walked into the shop to turn the gas out, stood in the doorway watching him. A smothered sigh as he glanced round the shop bore witness to the state of his feelings.

The jeweller hesitated again in the parlour, and then handing Brother Burge his candle turned out the gas, and led the way slowly upstairs to the room which had been prepared for the honoured visitor. He shook hands at the door and bade him an effusive good-night, his voice trembling despite himself as he expressed a hope that Mr. Burge would sleep well. He added casually that he himself was a very light sleeper.

To-night sleep of any kind was impossible. He had given up the front room to his guest, and his own window looked out on an over-grown garden. He sat trying to read, with his ears alert for the slightest sound. Brother Burge seemed to be a long time undressing. For half an hour after he had retired he could hear him moving restlessly about his room.

Twelve o'clock struck from the tower of the parish church, and was followed almost directly by the tall clock standing in the hall down-stairs. Scarcely had the sounds died away than a low moaning from the next room caused the affrighted jeweller to start from his chair and place his ear against the wall. Two or three hollow groans came through the plaster, followed by ejaculations which showed clearly that Brother Burge was at that moment engaged in a terrified combat with the Powers of Darkness to decide whether he should, or should not, rifle his host's shop. His hands clenched and his ear pressed close to the wall, the jeweller listened to a monologue which increased in interest with every word.

"I tell you I won't," said the voice in the next room with a groan, "I won't. Get thee behind me—Get thee—No, and don't shove me over to the door; if you can't get behind me without doing that, stay where you are. Yes, I know it's a fortune as well as what you do; but it ain't mine."

The listener caught his breath painfully.

"Diamond rings," continued Brother Burge in a suffocating voice. "Stop it, I tell you. No, I won't just go and look at 'em."

A series of groans which the jeweller noticed to his horror got weaker and weaker testified to the greatness of the temptation. He heard Brother Burge rise, and then a succession of panting snarls seemed to indicate a fierce bodily encounter.

"I don't—want to look at 'em," said Brother Burge in an exhausted voice. "What's—the good of—looking at 'em? It's like you, you know diamonds are my weakness. What does it matter if he is asleep? What's my knife got to do with you?"

Brother Higgs reeled back and a mist passed before his eyes. He came to himself at the sound of a door opening, and impelled with a vague idea of defending his property, snatched up his candle and looked out on to the landing.

The light fell on Brother Burge, fully dressed and holding his boots in his hand. For a moment they gazed at each other in silence; then the jeweller found his voice.

"I thought you were ill, Brother," he faltered.

An ugly scowl lit up the other's features. "Don't you tell me any of your lies," he said fiercely. "You're watching me; that's what you're doing. Spying on me."

"I thought that you were being tempted," confessed the trembling Mr. Higgs.

An expression of satisfaction which he strove to suppress appeared on Mr. Burge's face.

"So I was," he said sternly. "So I was; but that's my business. I don't want your assistance; I can fight my own battles. You go to bed—I'm going to tell the congregation I won the fight single-'anded."

"So you have, Brother," said the other eagerly; "but it's doing me good to see it. It's a lesson to me; a lesson to all of us the way you wrestled."

"I thought you was asleep," growled Brother Burge, turning back to his room and speaking over his shoulder. "You get back to bed; the fight ain't half over yet. Get back to bed and keep quiet."

The door closed behind him, and Mr. Higgs, still trembling, regained his room and looked in agony at the clock. It was only half-past twelve and the sun did not rise until six. He sat and shivered until a second instalment of groans in the next room brought him in desperation to his feet.

Brother Burge was in the toils again, and the jeweller despite his fears could not help realizing what a sensation the story of his temptation would create. Brother Burge was now going round and round his room like an animal in a cage, and sounds as of a soul wrought almost beyond endurance smote upon the listener's quivering ear. Then there was a long silence more alarming even than the noise of the conflict. Had Brother Burge won, and was he now sleeping the sleep of the righteous, or—Mr. Higgs shivered and put his other ear to the wall. Then he heard his guest move stealthily across the floor; the boards creaked and the handle of the door turned.

Mr. Higgs started, and with a sudden flash of courage born of anger and desperation seized a small brass poker from the fire-place, and taking the candle in his other hand went out on to the landing again. Brother Burge was closing his door softly, and his face when he turned it upon the jeweller was terrible in its wrath. His small eyes snapped with fury, and his huge hands opened and shut convulsively.

"What, agin!" he said in a low growl. "After all I told you!"

Mr. Higgs backed slowly as he advanced.

"No noise," said Mr. Burge in a dreadful whisper. "One scream and I'll— What were you going to do with that poker?"

He took a stealthy step forward.

"I—I," began the jeweller. His voice failed him. "Burglars," he mouthed, "downstairs."

"What?" said the other, pausing.

Mr. Higgs threw truth to the winds. "I heard them in the shop," he said, recovering, "that's why I took up the poker. Can't you hear them?"

Mr. Burge listened for the fraction of a second. "Nonsense," he said huskily.

"I heard them talking," said the other recklessly. "Let's go down and call the police."

"Call 'em from the winder," said Brother Burge, backing with some haste, "they might 'ave pistols or something, and they're ugly customers when they're disturbed."

He stood with strained face listening.

"Here they come," whispered the jeweller with a sudden movement of alarm.

Brother Burge turned, and bolting into his room clapped the door to and locked it. The jeweller stood dumbfounded on the landing; then he heard the window go up and the voice of Brother Burge, much strengthened by the religious exercises of the past six months, bellowing lustily for the police.

For a few seconds Mr. Higgs stood listening and wondering what explanation he should give. Still thinking, he ran downstairs, and, throwing open the pantry window, unlocked the door leading into the shop and scattered a few of his cherished possessions about the floor. By the time he had done this, people were already beating upon the street-door and exchanging hurried remarks with Mr. Burge at the window above. The jeweller shot back the bolts, and half-a-dozen neighbours, headed by the butcher opposite, clad in his nightgown and armed with a cleaver, burst into the passage. A constable came running up just as the pallid face of Brother Burge peered over the balusters. The constable went upstairs three at a time, and twisting his hand in the ex-burglar's neck-cloth bore him backwards.

"I've got one," he shouted. "Come up and hold him while I look round."

The butcher was beside him in a moment; Brother Burge struggling wildly, called loudly upon the name of Brother Higgs.

"That's all right, constable," said the latter, "that's a friend of mine."

"Friend o' yours, sir?" said the disappointed officer, still holding him.

The jeweller nodded. "Mr. Samuel Burge the Converted Burglar," he said mechanically.

"Conver—" gasped the astonished constable. "Converted burglar? Here!"

"He is a preacher now," added Mr. Higgs.

"Preacher?" retorted the constable. "Why it's as plain as a pikestaff. Confederates: his part was to go down and let 'em in."

Mr. Burge raised a piteous outcry. "I hope you may be forgiven for them words," he cried piously.

"What time did you go up to bed?" pursued the constable.

"About half-past eleven," replied Mr. Higgs.

The other grunted with satisfaction. "And he's fully dressed, with his boots off," he remarked. "Did you hear him go out of his room at all?"

"He did go out," said the jeweller truth-fully, "but—"

"I thought so," said the constable, turning to his prisoner with affectionate solicitude. "Now you come along o' me. Come quietly, because it'll be the best for you in the end."

"You won't get your skull split open then," added the butcher, toying with his cleaver.

The jeweller hesitated. He had no desire to be left alone with Mr. Burge again; and a sense of humour, which many years' association with the Primitive Apostles had not quite eradicated, strove for hearing.

"Think of the sermon it'll make," he said encouragingly to the frantic Mr. Burge, "think of the congregation!"

Brother Burge replied in language which he had not used in public since he had joined the Apostles. The butcher and another man stood guard over him while the constable searched the premises and made all secure again. Then with a final appeal to Mr. Higgs who was keeping in the background, he was pitched to the police-station by the energetic constable and five zealous assistants.

A diffidence, natural in the circumstances, prevented him from narrating the story of his temptation to the magistrates next morning, and Mr. Higgs was equally reticent. He was put back while the police communicated with London, and in the meantime Brother Clark and a band of Apostles flanked down to his support.

On his second appearance before the magistrates he was confronted with his past; and his past to the great astonishment of the Brethren being free from all blemish with the solitary exception of fourteen days for stealing milk-cans, he was discharged with a caution. The disillusioned Primitive Apostles also gave him his freedom.

THE TEST

Pebblesea was dull, and Mr. Frederick Dix, mate of the ketch Starfish, after a long and unsuccessful quest for amusement, returned to the harbor with an idea of forgetting his disappointment in sleep. The few shops in the High Street were closed, and the only entertainment offered at the taverns was contained in glass and pewter.

The attitude of the landlord of the "Pilots' Hope," where Mr. Dix had sought to enliven the proceedings by a song and dance, still rankled in his memory.

The skipper and the hands were still ashore and the ketch looked so lonely that the mate, thinking better of his idea of retiring, thrust his hands deep in his pockets and sauntered round the harbor. It was nearly dark, and the only other man visible stood at the edge of the quay gazing at the water. He stood for so long that the mate's easily aroused curiosity awoke, and, after twice passing, he edged up to him and ventured a remark on the fineness of the night.

"The night's all right," said the young man, gloomily.

"You're rather near the edge," said the mate, after a pause.

"I like being near the edge," was the reply.

Mr. Dix whistled softly and, glancing up at the tall, white-faced young man before him, pushed his cap back and scratched his head.

"Ain't got anything on your mind, have you?" he inquired.

The young man groaned and turned away, and the mate, scenting a little excitement, took him gently by the coat-sleeve and led him from the brink. Sympathy begets confidence, and, within the next ten minutes, he had learned that Arthur Heard, rejected by Emma Smith, was contemplating the awful crime of self-destruction.

"Why, I've known 'er for seven years," said Mr. Heard; "seven years, and this is the end of it."

The mate shook his head.

"I told er I was coming straight away to drownd myself," pursued Mr. Heard. "My last words to 'er was, 'When you see my bloated corpse you'll be sorry.'"

"I expect she'll cry and carry on like anything," said the mate, politely.

The other turned and regarded him. "Why, you don't think I'm going to, do you?" he inquired, sharply. "Why, I wouldn't drownd myself for fifty blooming gells."

"But what did you tell her you were going to for, then?" demanded the puzzled mate.

"'Cos I thought it would upset 'er and make 'er give way," said the other, bitterly; "and all it done was to make 'er laugh as though she'd 'ave a fit."

"It would serve her jolly well right if you did drown yourself," said Mr. Dix, judiciously. "It 'ud spoil her life for her."

"Ah, and it wouldn't spoil mine, I s'pose?" rejoined Mr. Heard, with ferocious sarcasm.

"How she will laugh when she sees you to-morrow," mused the mate. "Is she the sort of girl that would spread it about?"

Mr. Heard said that she was, and, forgetting for a moment his great love, referred to her partiality for gossip in the most scathing terms he could muster. The mate, averse to such a tame ending to a promising adventure, eyed him thoughtfully.

"Why not just go in and out again," he said, seductively, "and run to her house all dripping wet?"

"That would be clever, wouldn't it?" said the ungracious Mr. Heard. "Starting to commit suicide, and then thinking better of it. Why, I should be a bigger laughing-stock than ever."

"But suppose I saved you against your will?" breathed the tempter; "how would that be?"

"It would be all right if I cared to run the risk," said the other, "but I don't. I should look well struggling in the water while you was diving in the wrong places for me, shouldn't I?"

"I wasn't thinking of such a thing," said Mr. Dix, hastily; "twenty strokes is about my mark—with my clothes off. My idea was to pull you out."

Mr. Heard glanced at the black water a dozen feet below. "How?" he inquired, shortly.

"Not here," said the mate. "Come to the end of the quay where the ground slopes to the water. It's shallow there, and you can tell her that you jumped in off here. She won't know the difference."

With an enthusiasm which Mr. Heard made no attempt to share, he led the way to the place indicated, and dilating upon its manifold advantages, urged him to go in at once and get it over.

"You couldn't have a better night for it," he said, briskly. "Why, it makes me feel like a dip myself to look at it."

Mr. Heard gave a surly grunt, and after testing the temperature of the water with his hand, slowly and reluctantly immersed one foot. Then, with sudden resolution, he waded in and, ducking his head, stood up gasping.

"Give yourself a good soaking while you're about it," said the delighted mate.

Mr. Heard ducked again, and once more emerging stumbled towards the bank.

"Pull me out," he cried, sharply.

Mr. Dix, smiling indulgently, extended his hands, which Mr. Heard seized with the proverbial grasp of a drowning man.

"All right, take it easy, don't get excited," said the smiling mate, "four foot of water won't hurt anyone. If—Here! Let go o' me, d'ye hear? Let go! If you don't let go I'll punch your head."

"You couldn't save me against my will without coming in," said Mr. Heard. "Now we can tell 'er you dived in off the quay and got me just as I was sinking for the last time. You'll be a hero."

The mate's remarks about heroes were mercifully cut short. He was three stone lighter than Mr. Heard, and standing on shelving ground. The latter's victory was so sudden that he over-balanced, and only a commotion at the surface of the water showed where they had disappeared.

Mr. Heard was first up and out, but almost immediately the figure of the mate, who had gone under with his mouth open, emerged from the water and crawled ashore.

"You—wait—till I—get my breath back," he gasped.

"There's no ill-feeling, I 'ope?" said Mr. Heard, anxiously. "I'll tell everybody of your bravery. Don't spoil everything for the sake of a little temper."

Mr. Dix stood up and clinched his fists, but at the spectacle of the dripping, forlorn figure before him his wrath vanished and he broke into a hearty laugh.

"Come on, mate," he said, clapping him on the back, "now let's go and find Emma. If she don't fall in love with you now she never will. My eye! you are a picture!"

He began to walk towards the town, and Mr. Heard, with his legs wide apart and his arms held stiffly from his body, waddled along beside him. Two little streamlets followed.

They walked along the quay in silence, and had nearly reached the end of it, when the figure of a man turned the corner of the houses and advanced at a shambling trot towards them.

"Old Smith!" said Mr. Heard, in a hasty whisper. "Now, be careful. Hold me tight."

The new-comer thankfully dropped into a walk as he saw them, and came to a standstill with a cry of astonishment as the light of a neighboring lamp revealed their miserable condition.

"Wot, Arthur!" he exclaimed.

"Halloa," said Mr. Heard, drearily.

"The idea o' your being so sinful," said Mr. Smith, severely. "Emma told me wot you said, but I never thought as you'd got the pluck to go and do it. I'm surprised at you."

"I ain't done it," said Mr. Heard, in a sullen voice; "nobody can drown themselves in comfort with a lot of interfering people about."

Mr. Smith turned and gazed at the mate, and a broad beam of admiration shone in his face as he grasped that gentleman's hand.

"Come into the 'ouse both of you and get some dry clothes," he said, warmly.

He thrust his strong, thick-set figure between them, and with a hand on each coat-collar propelled them in the direction of home. The mate muttered something about going back to his ship, but Mr. Smith refused to listen, and stopping at the door of a neat cottage, turned the handle and thrust his dripping charges over the threshold of a comfortable sitting-room.

A pleasant-faced woman of middle age and a pretty girl of twenty rose at their entrance, and a faint scream fell pleasantly upon the ears of Mr. Heard.

"Here he is," bawled Mr. Smith; "just saved at the last moment."

"What, two of them?" exclaimed Miss Smith, with a faint note of gratification in her voice. Her gaze fell on the mate, and she smiled approvingly.

"No; this one jumped in and saved 'im," said her father.

"Oh, Arthur!" said Miss Smith. "How could you be so wicked! I never dreamt you'd go and do such a thing—never! I didn't think you'd got it in you."

Mr. Heard grinned sheepishly. "I told you I would," he muttered.

"Don't stand talking here," said Mrs. Smith, gazing at the puddle which was growing in the centre of the carpet; "they'll catch cold. Take 'em upstairs and give 'em some dry clothes. And I'll bring some hot whisky and water up to 'em."

"Rum is best," said Mr. Smith, herding his charges and driving them up the small staircase. "Send young Joe for some. Send up three glasses." They disappeared upstairs, and Joe appearing at that moment from the kitchen, was hastily sent off to the "Blue Jay" for the rum. A couple of curious neighbors helped him to carry it back, and, standing modestly just inside the door, ventured on a few skilled directions as to its preparation. After which, with an eye on Miss Smith, they stood and conversed, mostly in head-shakes.

Stimulated by the rum and the energetic Mr. Smith, the men were not long in changing. Preceded by their host, they came down to the sitting-room again; Mr. Heard with as desperate and unrepentant an air as he could assume, and Mr. Dix trying to conceal his uneasiness by taking great interest in a suit of clothes three sizes too large for him.

"They was both as near drownded as could be," said Mr. Smith, looking round; "he ses Arthur fought like a madman to prevent 'imself from being saved."

"It was nothing, really," said the mate, in an almost inaudible voice, as he met Miss Smith's admiring gaze.

"Listen to 'im," said the delighted Mr. Smith; "all brave men are like that. That's wot's made us Englishmen wot we are."

"I don't suppose he knew who it was he was saving," said a voice from the door.

"I didn't want to be saved," said Mr. Heard, defiantly.

"Well, you can easy do it again, Arthur," said the same voice; "the dock won't run away."

Mr. Heard started and eyed the speaker with same malevolence.

"Tell us all about it," said Miss Smith, gazing at the mate, with her hands clasped. "Did you see him jump in?"

Mr. Dix shook his head and looked at Mr. Heard for guidance. "N—not exactly," he stammered; "I was just taking a stroll round the harbor before turning in, when all of a sudden I heard a cry for help—"

"No you didn't," broke in Mr. Heard, fiercely.

"Well, it sounded like it," said the mate, somewhat taken aback.

"I don't care what it sounded like," said the other. "I didn't say it. It was the last thing I should 'ave called out. I didn't want to be saved."

"P'r'aps he cried 'Emma,'" said the voice from the door.

"Might ha' been that," admitted the mate. "Well, when I heard it I ran to the edge and looked down at the water, and at first I couldn't see anything. Then I saw what I took to be a dog, but, knowing that dogs can't cry 'help!'—"

"Emma," corrected Mr. Heard.

"Emma," said the mate, "I just put my hands up and dived in. When I came to the surface I struck out for him and tried to seize him from behind, but before I could do so he put his arms round my neck like—like—"

"Like as if it was Emma's," suggested the voice by the door.

Miss Smith rose with majestic dignity and confronted the speaker. "And who asked you in here, George Harris?" she inquired, coldly.

"I see the door open," stammered Mr. Harris—"I see the door open and I thought—"

"If you look again you'll see the handle," said Miss Smith.

Mr. Harris looked, and, opening the door with extreme care, melted slowly from a gaze too terrible for human endurance.

"We went down like a stone," continued the mate, as Miss Smith resumed her seat and smiled at him. "When we came up he tried to get away again. I think we went down again a few more times, but I ain't sure. Then we crawled out; leastways I did, and pulled him after me."

"He might have drowned you," said Miss Smith, with a severe glance at her unfortunate admirer. "And it's my belief that he tumbled in after all, and when you thought he was struggling to get away he was struggling to be saved. That's more like him."

"Well, they're all right now," said Mr. Smith, as Mr. Heard broke in with some vehemence. "And this chap's going to 'ave the Royal Society's medal for it, or I'll know the reason why."

"No, no," said the mate, hurriedly; "I wouldn't take it, I couldn't think of it."

"Take it or leave it," said Mr. Smith; "but I'm going to the police to try and get it for you. I know the inspector a bit."

"I can't take it," said the horrified mate; "it—it—besides, don't you see, if this isn't kept quiet Mr. Heard will be locked up for trying to commit suicide."

"So he would be," said the other man from his post by the door; "he's quite right."

"And I'd sooner lose fifty medals," said Mr. Dix. "What's the good of me saving him for that?"

A murmur of admiration at the mate's extraordinary nobility of character jarred harshly on the ears of Mr. Heard. Most persistent of all was the voice of Miss Smith, and hardly able to endure things quietly, he sat and watched the tender glances which passed between her and Mr. Dix. Miss Smith, conscious at last of his regards, turned and looked at him.

"You could say you tumbled in, Arthur, and then he would get the medal," she said, softly.

"Say!" shouted the overwrought Mr. Heard. "Say I tum—"

Words failed him. He stood swaying and regarding the company for a moment, and then, flinging open the door, closed it behind him with a bang that made the house tremble.

The mate followed half an hour later, escorted to the ship by the entire Smith family. Fortified by the presence of Miss Smith, he pointed out the exact scene of the rescue without a tremor, and, when her father narrated the affair to the skipper, whom they found sitting on deck smoking a last pipe, listened undismayed to that astonished mariner's comments.

News of the mate's heroic conduct became general the next day, and work on the ketch was somewhat impeded in consequence. It became a point of honor with Mr. Heard's fellow-townsmen to allude to the affair as an accident, but the romantic nature of the transaction was well understood, and full credit given to Mr. Dix for his self-denial in the matter of the medal. Small boys followed him in the street, and half Pebblesea knew when he paid a visit to the Smith's, and discussed his chances. Two nights afterwards, when he and Miss Smith went for a walk in the loneliest spot they could find, conversation turned almost entirely upon the over-crowded condition of the British Isles.

The Starfish was away for three weeks, but the little town no longer looked dull to the mate as she entered the harbor one evening and glided slowly towards her old berth. Emma Smith was waiting to see the ship come in, and his taste for all other amusements had temporarily disappeared.

For two or three days the course of true love ran perfectly smooth; then, like a dark shadow, the figure of Arthur Heard was thrown across its path. It haunted the quay, hung about the house, and cropped up unexpectedly in the most distant solitudes. It came up behind the mate one evening just as he left the ship and walked beside him in silence.

"Halloa," said the mate, at last.

"Halloa," said Mr. Heard. "Going to see Emma?"

"I'm going to see Miss Smith," said the mate.

Mr. Heard laughed; a forced, mirthless laugh.

"And we don't want you following us about," said Mr. Dix, sharply. "If it'll ease your mind, and do you any good to know, you never had a chance. She told me so."

"I sha'n't follow you," said Mr. Heard; "it's your last evening, so you'd better make the most of it."

He turned on his heel, and the mate, pondering on his last words, went thoughtfully on to the house.

Amid the distraction of pleasant society and a long walk, the matter passed from his mind, and he only remembered it at nine o'clock that evening as a knock sounded on the door and the sallow face of Mr. Heard was thrust into the room.

"Good-evening all," said the intruder.

"Evening, Arthur," said Mr. Smith, affably.

Mr. Heard with a melancholy countenance entered the room and closed the door gently behind him. Then he coughed slightly and shook his head.

"Anything the matter, Arthur?" inquired Mr. Smith, somewhat disturbed by these manifestations.

"I've got something on my mind," said Mr. Heard, with a diabolical glance at the mate—"something wot's been worrying me for a long time. I've been deceiving you."

"That was always your failing, Arthur—deceitfulness," said Mrs. Smith. "I remember—"

"We've both been deceiving you," interrupted Mr. Heard, loudly. "I didn't jump into the harbor the other night, and I didn't tumble in, and Mr. Fred Dix didn't jump in after me; we just went to the end of the harbor and walked in and wetted ourselves."

There was a moment's intense silence and all eyes turned on the mate. The latter met them boldly.

"It's a habit o' mine to walk into the water and spoil my clothes for the sake of people I've never met before," he said, with a laugh.

"For shame, Arthur!" said Mr. Smith, with a huge sigh of relief.

"'Ow can you?" said Mrs. Smith.

"Arthur's been asleep since then," said the mate, still smiling. "All the same, the next time he jumps in he can get out by himself."

Mr. Heard, raising his voice, entered into a minute description of the affair, but in vain. Mr. Smith, rising to his feet, denounced his ingratitude in language which was seldom allowed to pass unchallenged in the presence of his wife, while that lady contributed examples of deceitfulness in the past of Mr. Heard, which he strove in vain to refute. Meanwhile, her daughter patted the mate's hand.

"It's a bit too thin, Arthur," said the latter, with a mocking smile; "try something better next time."

"Very well," said Mr. Heard, in quieter tones; "I dare you to come along to the harbor and jump in, just as you are, where you said you jumped in after me. They'll soon see who's telling the truth."

"He'll do that," said Mr. Smith, with conviction.

For a fraction of a second Mr. Dix hesitated, then, with a steady glance at Miss Smith, he sprang to his feet and accepted the challenge. Mrs. Smith besought him not to be foolish, and, with a vague idea of dissuading him, told him a slanderous anecdote concerning Mr. Heard's aunt. Her daughter gazed at the mate with proud confidence, and, taking his arm, bade her mother to get some dry clothes ready and led the way to the harbor.

The night was fine but dark, and a chill breeze blew up from the sea. Twice the hapless mate thought of backing out, but a glance at Miss Smith's profile and the tender pressure of her arm deterred him. The tide was running out and he had a faint hope that he might keep afloat long enough to be washed ashore alive. He talked rapidly, and his laugh rang across the water. Arrived at the spot they stopped, and Miss Smith looking down into the darkness was unable to repress a shiver.

"Be careful, Fred," she said, laying her hand upon his arm.

The mate looked at her oddly. "All right," he said, gayly, "I'll be out almost before I'm in. You run back to the house and help your mother get the dry clothes ready for me."

His tones were so confident, and his laugh so buoyant, that Mr. Heard, who had been fully expecting him to withdraw from the affair, began to feel that he had under-rated his swimming powers. "Just jumping in and swimming out again is not quite the same as saving a drownding man," he said, with a sneer.

In a flash the mate saw a chance of escape.

"Why, there's no satisfying you," he said, slowly. "If I do go in I can see that you won't own up that you've been lying."

"He'll 'ave to," said Mr. Smith, who, having made up his mind for a little excitement, was in no mind to lose it.

"I don't believe he would," said the mate. "Look here!" he said, suddenly, as he laid an affectionate arm on the old man's shoulder. "I know what we'll do."

"Well?" said Mr. Smith.

"I'll save you," said the mate, with a smile of great relief.

"Save me?" said the puzzled Mr. Smith, as his daughter uttered a faint cry. "How?"

"Just as I saved him," said the other, nodding. "You jump in, and after you've sunk twice—same as he did—I'll dive in and save you. At any rate I'll do my best; I promise you I won't come ashore without you."

Mr. Smith hastily flung off the encircling arm and retired a few paces inland. "'Ave you—ever been—in a lunatic asylum at any time?" he inquired, as soon as he could speak.

"No," said the mate, gravely.

"Neither 'ave I," said Mr. Smith; "and, what's more, I'm not going."

He took a deep breath and stood simmering. Miss Smith came forward and, with a smothered giggle, took the mate's arm and squeezed it.

"It'll have to be Arthur again, then," said the latter, in a resigned voice.

"Me?" cried Mr. Heard, with a start.

"Yes, you!" said the mate, in a decided voice. "After what you said just now I'm not going in without saving somebody. It would be no good. Come on, in you go."

"He couldn't speak fairer than that, Arthur," said Mr. Smith, dispassionately, as he came forward again.

"But I tell you he can't swim," protested Mr. Heard, "not properly. He didn't swim last time; I told you so."

"Never mind; we know what you said," retorted the mate. "All you've got to do is to jump in and I'll follow and save you—same as I did the other night."

"Go on, Arthur," said Mr. Smith, encouragingly. "It ain't cold."

"I tell you he can't swim," repeated Mr. Heard, passionately. "I should be drownded before your eyes."

"Rubbish," said Mr. Smith. "Why, I believe you're afraid."

"I should be drownded, I tell you," said Mr. Heard. "He wouldn't come in after me."

"Yes, he would," said Mr. Smith, passing a muscular arm round the mate's waist; "'cos the moment you're overboard I'll drop 'im in. Are you ready?"

He stood embracing the mate and waiting, but Mr. Heard, with an infuriated exclamation, walked away. A parting glance showed him that the old man had released the mate, and that the latter was now embracing Miss Smith.

THE THREE SISTERS

Thirty years ago on a wet autumn evening the household of Mallett's Lodge was gathered round the death-bed of Ursula Mallow, the eldest of the three sisters who inhabited it. The dingy moth-eaten curtains of the old wooden bedstead were drawn apart, the light of a smoking oil-lamp falling upon the hopeless countenance of the dying woman as she turned her dull eyes upon her sisters. The room was in silence except for an occasional sob from the youngest sister, Eunice. Outside the rain fell steadily over the steaming marshes.

"Nothing is to be changed, Tabitha," gasped Ursula to the other sister, who bore a striking likeness to her although her expression was harder and colder; "this room is to be locked up and never opened."

"Very well," said Tabitha brusquely, "though I don't see how it can matter to you then."

"It does matter," said her sister with startling energy. "How do you know, how do I know that I may not sometimes visit it? I have lived in this house so long I am certain that I shall see it again. I will come back. Come back to watch over you both and see that no harm befalls you."

"You are talking wildly," said Tabitha, by no means moved at her sister's solicitude for her welfare. "Your mind is wandering; you know that I have no faith in such things."

Ursula sighed, and beckoning to Eunice, who was weeping silently at the bedside, placed her feeble arms around her neck and kissed her.

"Do not weep, dear," she said feebly. "Perhaps it is best so. A lonely woman's life is scarce worth living. We have no hopes, no aspirations; other women have had happy husbands and children, but we in this forgotten place have grown old together. I go first, but you must soon follow."

Tabitha, comfortably conscious of only forty years and an iron frame, shrugged her shoulders and smiled grimly.

"I go first." repeated Ursula in a new and strange voice as her heavy eyes slowly closed, "but I will come for each of you in turn, when your lease of life runs out. At that moment I will be with you to lead your steps whither I now go."

As she spoke the flickering lamp went out suddenly as though extinguished by a rapid hand, and the room was left in utter darkness. A strange suffocating noise issued from the bed, and when the trembling women had relighted the lamp, all that was left of Ursula Mallow was ready for the grave.

That night the survivors passed together. The dead woman had been a firm believer in the existence of that shadowy borderland which is said to form an unhallowed link between the living and the dead, and even the stolid Tabitha, slightly unnerved by the events of the night, was not free from certain apprehensions that she might have been right.

With the bright morning their fears disappeared. The sun stole in at the window, and seeing the poor earth-worn face on the pillow so touched it and glorified it that only its goodness and weakness were seen, and the beholders came to wonder how they could ever have felt any dread of aught so calm and peaceful. A day or two passed, and the body was transferred to a massive coffin long regarded as the finest piece of work of its kind ever turned out of the village carpenter's workshop. Then a slow and melancholy cortege headed by four bearers wound its solemn way across the marshes to the family vault in the grey old church, and all that was left of Ursula was placed by the father and mother who had taken that self-same journey some thirty years before.

To Eunice as they toiled slowly home the day seemed strange and Sabbath-like, the flat prospect of marsh wilder and more forlorn than usual, the roar of the sea more depressing. Tabitha had no such fancies. The bulk of the dead woman's property had been left to Eunice, and her avaricious soul was sorely troubled and her proper sisterly feelings of regret for the deceased sadly interfered with in consequence.

"What are you going to do with all that money, Eunice?" she asked as they sat at their quiet tea.

"I shall leave it as it stands," said Eunice slowly. "We have both got sufficient to live upon, and I shall devote the income from it to supporting some beds in a children's hospital."

"If Ursula had wished it to go to a hospital," said Tabitha in her deep tones, "she would have left the money to it herself. I wonder you do not respect her wishes more."

"What else can I do with it then?" inquired Eunice.

"Save it," said the other with gleaming eyes, "save it."

Eunice shook her head.

"No," said she, "it shall go to the sick children, but the principal I will not touch, and if I die before you it shall become yours and you can do what you like with it."

"Very well," said Tabitha, smothering her anger by a strong effort; "I don't believe that was what Ursula meant you to do with it, and I don't believe she will rest quietly in the grave while you squander the money she stored so carefully."

"What do you mean?" asked Eunice with pale lips. "You are trying to frighten me; I thought that you did not believe in such things."

Tabitha made no answer, and to avoid the anxious inquiring gaze of her sister, drew her chair to the fire, and folding her gaunt arms, composed herself for a nap.

For some time life went on quietly in the old house. The room of the dead woman, in accordance with her last desire, was kept firmly locked, its dirty windows forming a strange contrast to the prim cleanliness of the others. Tabitha, never very talkative, became more taciturn than ever, and stalked about the house and the neglected garden like an unquiet spirit, her brow roughened into the deep wrinkles suggestive of much thought. As the winter came on, bringing with it the long dark evenings, the old house became more lonely than ever, and an air of mystery and dread seemed to hang over it and brood in its empty rooms and dark corridors. The deep silence of night was broken by strange noises for which neither the wind nor the rats could be held accountable. Old Martha, seated in her distant kitchen, heard strange sounds upon the stairs, and once, upon hurrying to them, fancied that she saw a dark figure squatting upon the landing, though a subsequent search with candle and spectacles failed to discover anything. Eunice was disturbed by several vague incidents, and, as she suffered from a complaint of the heart, rendered very ill by them. Even Tabitha admitted a strangeness about the house, but, confident in her piety and virtue, took no heed of it, her mind being fully employed in another direction.

Since the death of her sister all restraint upon her was removed, and she yielded herself up entirely to the stern and hard rules enforced by avarice upon its devotees. Her housekeeping expenses were kept rigidly separate from those of Eunice and her food limited to the coarsest dishes, while in the matter of clothes, the old servant was by far the better dressed. Seated alone in her bedroom this uncouth, hard-featured creature revelled in her possessions, grudging even the expense of the candle-end which enabled her to behold them. So completely did this passion change her that both Eunice and Martha became afraid of her, and lay awake in their beds night after night trembling at the chinking of the coins at her unholy vigils.

One day Eunice ventured to remonstrate. "Why don't you bank your money, Tabitha?" she said; "it is surely not safe to keep such large sums in such a lonely house."

"Large sums!" repeated the exasperated Tabitha, "large sums! what nonsense is this? You know well that I have barely sufficient to keep me."

"It's a great temptation to housebreakers," said her sister, not pressing the point. "I made sure last night that I heard somebody in the house."

"Did you?" said Tabitha, grasping her arm, a horrible look on her face. "So did I. I thought they went to Ursula's room, and I got out of bed and went on the stairs to listen."

"Well?" said Eunice faintly, fascinated by the look on her sister's face.

"There was something there," said Tabitha slowly. "I'll swear it, for I stood on the landing by her door and listened; something scuffling on the floor round and round the room. At first I thought it was the cat, but when I went up there this morning the door was still locked, and the cat was in the kitchen."

"Oh, let us leave this dreadful house," moaned Eunice.

"What!" said her sister grimly; "afraid of poor Ursula? Why should you be? Your own sister who nursed you when you were a babe, and who perhaps even now comes and watches over your slumbers."

"Oh!" said Eunice, pressing her hand to her side, "if I saw her I should die. I should think that she had come for me as she said she would. O God! have mercy on me, I am dying."

She reeled as she spoke, and before Tabitha could save her, sank senseless to the floor.

"Get some water," cried Tabitha, as old Martha came hurrying up the stairs, "Eunice has fainted."

The old woman, with a timid glance at her, retired, reappearing shortly afterwards with the water, with which she proceeded to restore her much-loved mistress to her senses. Tabitha, as soon as this was accomplished, stalked off to her room, leaving her sister and Martha sitting drearily enough in the small parlour, watching the fire and conversing in whispers.

It was clear to the old servant that this state of things could not last much longer, and she repeatedly urged her mistress to leave a house so lonely and so mysterious. To her great delight Eunice at length consented, despite the fierce opposition of her sister, and at the mere idea of leaving gained greatly in health and spirits. A small but comfortable house was hired in Morville, and arrangements made for a speedy change.

It was the last night in the old house, and all the wild spirits of the marshes, the wind and the sea seemed to have joined forces for one supreme effort. When the wind dropped, as it did at brief intervals, the sea was heard moaning on the distant beach, strangely mingled with the desolate warning of the bell-buoy as it rocked to the waves. Then the wind rose again, and the noise of the sea was lost in the fierce gusts which, finding no obstacle on the open marshes, swept with their full fury upon the house by the creek. The strange voices of the air shrieked in its chimneys windows rattled, doors slammed, and even, the very curtains seemed to live and move.

Eunice was in bed, awake. A small nightlight in a saucer of oil shed a sickly glare upon the worm-eaten old furniture, distorting the most innocent articles into ghastly shapes. A wilder gust than usual almost deprived her of the protection afforded by that poor light, and she lay listening fearfully to the creakings and other noises on the stairs, bitterly regretting that she had not asked Martha to sleep with her. But it was not too late even now. She slipped hastily to the floor, crossed to the huge wardrobe, and was in the very act of taking her dressing-gown from its peg when an unmistakable footfall was heard on the stairs. The robe dropped from her shaking fingers, and with a quickly beating heart she regained her bed.

The sounds ceased and a deep silence followed, which she herself was unable to break although she strove hard to do so. A wild gust of wind shook the windows and nearly extinguished the light, and when its flame had regained its accustomed steadiness she saw that the door was slowly opening, while the huge shadow of a hand blotted the papered wall. Still her tongue refused its office. The door flew open with a crash, a cloaked figure entered and, throwing aside its coverings, she saw with a horror past all expression the napkin-bound face of the dead Ursula smiling terribly at her. In her last extremity she raised her faded eyes above for succour, and then as the figure noiselessly advanced and laid its cold hand upon her brow, the soul of Eunice Mallow left its body with a wild shriek and made its way to the Eternal.

Martha, roused by the cry, and shivering with dread, rushed to the door and gazed in terror at the figure which stood leaning over the bedside. As she watched, it slowly removed the cowl and the napkin and exposed the fell face of Tabitha, so strangely contorted between fear and triumph that she hardly recognized it.

"Who's there?" cried Tabitha in a terrible voice as she saw the old woman's shadow on the wall.

"I thought I heard a cry," said Martha, entering. "Did anybody call?"

"Yes, Eunice," said the other, regarding her closely. "I, too, heard the cry, and hurried to her. What makes her so strange? Is she in a trance?"

"Ay," said the old woman, falling on her knees by the bed and sobbing bitterly, "the trance of death. Ah, my dear, my poor lonely girl, that this should be the end of it! She has died of fright," said the old woman, pointing to the eyes, which even yet retained their horror. "She has seen something devilish."

Tabitha's gaze fell. "She has always suffered with her heart," she muttered; "the night has frightened her; it frightened me."

She stood upright by the foot of the bed as Martha drew the sheet over the face of the dead woman.

"First Ursula, then Eunice," said Tabitha, drawing a deep breath. "I can't stay here. I'll dress and wait for the morning."

She left the room as she spoke, and with bent head proceeded to her own. Martha remained by the bedside, and gently closing the staring eyes, fell on her knees, and prayed long and earnestly for the departed soul. Overcome with grief and fear she remained with bowed head until a sudden sharp cry from Tabitha brought her to her feet.

"Well," said the old woman, going to the door.

"Where are you?" cried Tabitha, somewhat reassured by her voice.

"In Miss Eunice's bedroom. Do you want anything?"

"Come down at once. Quick! I am unwell."

Her voice rose suddenly to a scream. "Quick! For God's sake! Quick, or I shall go mad. There is some strange woman in the house."

The old woman stumbled hastily down the dark stairs. "What is the matter?" she cried, entering the room. "Who is it? What do you mean?"

"I saw it," said Tabitha, grasping her convulsively by the shoulder. "I was coming to you when I saw the figure of a woman in front of me going up the stairs. Is it—can it be Ursula come for the soul of Eunice, as she said she would?"

"Or for yours?" said Martha, the words coming from her in some odd fashion, despite herself.

Tabitha, with a ghastly look, fell cowering by her side, clutching tremulously at her clothes. "Light the lamps," she cried hysterically. "Light a fire, make a noise; oh, this dreadful darkness! Will it never be day!"

"Soon, soon," said Martha, overcoming her repugnance and trying to pacify her. "When the day comes you will laugh at these fears."

"I murdered her," screamed the miserable woman, "I killed her with fright. Why did she not give me the money? 'Twas no use to her. Ah! Look there!"

Martha, with a horrible fear, followed her glance to the door, but saw nothing.

"It's Ursula," said Tabitha from between her teeth. "Keep her off! Keep her off!"

The old woman, who by some unknown sense seemed to feel the presence of a third person in the room, moved a step forward and stood before her. As she did so Tabitha waved her arms as though to free herself from the touch of a detaining hand, half rose to her feet, and without a word fell dead before her.

At this the old woman's courage forsook her, and with a great cry she rushed from the room, eager to escape from this house of death and mystery. The bolts of the great door were stiff with age, and strange voices seemed to ring in her ears as she strove wildly to unfasten them. Her brain whirled. She thought that the dead in their distant rooms called to her, and that a devil stood on the step outside laughing and holding the door against her. Then with a supreme effort she flung it open, and heedless of her night-clothes passed into the bitter night. The path across the marshes was lost in the darkness, but she found it; the planks over the ditches slippery and narrow, but she crossed them in safety, until at last, her feet bleeding and her breath coming in great gasps, she entered the village and sank down more dead than alive on a cottage doorstep.

TO HAVE AND TO HOLD

The old man sat outside the Cauliflower Inn, looking crossly up the road. He was fond of conversation, but the pedestrian who had stopped to drink a mug of ale beneath the shade of the doors was not happy in his choice of subjects. He would only talk of the pernicious effects of beer on the constitutions of the aged, and he listened with ill-concealed impatience to various points which the baffled ancient opposite urged in its favour.

Conversation languished; the traveller rapped on the table and had his mug refilled. He nodded courteously to his companion and drank.

"Seems to me," said the latter, sharply, "you like it for all your talk."

The other shook his head gently, and, leaning back, bestowed a covert wink upon the signboard. He then explained that it was the dream of his life to give up beer.

"You're another Job Brown," said the old man, irritably, "that's wot you are; another Job Brown. I've seen your kind afore."

He shifted farther along the seat, and, taking up his long clay pipe from the table, struck a match and smoked the few whiffs which remained. Then he heard the traveller order a pint of ale with gin in it and a paper of tobacco. His dull eyes glistened, but he made a feeble attempt to express surprise when these luxuries were placed before him.

"Wot I said just now about you being like Job Brown was only in joke like," he said, anxiously, as he tasted the brew. "If Job 'ad been like you he'd ha' been a better man."

The philanthropist bowed. He also manifested a little curiosity concerning one to whom he had, for however short a time, suggested a resemblance.

"He was one o' the 'ardest drinkers in these parts," began the old man, slowly, filling his pipe.

The traveller thanked him.

"Wot I meant was"—said the old man, hastily—"that all the time 'e was drinking 'e was talking agin beer same as you was just now, and he used to try all sorts o' ways and plans of becoming a teetotaler. He used to sit up 'ere of a night drinking 'is 'ardest and talking all the time of ways and means by which 'e could give it up. He used to talk about hisself as if 'e was somebody else 'e was trying to do good to.

The chaps about 'ere got sick of 'is talk. They was poor men mostly, same as they are now, and they could only drink a little ale now and then; an' while they was doing of it they 'ad to sit and listen to Job Brown, who made lots o' money dealing, drinking pint arter pint o' gin and beer and calling it pison, an' saying they was killing theirselves.

"Sometimes 'e used to get pitiful over it, and sit shaking 'is 'ead at 'em for drowning theirselves in beer, as he called it, when they ought to be giving the money to their wives and families. He sat down and cried one night over Bill Chambers's wife's toes being out of 'er boots. Bill sat struck all of a 'eap, and it might 'ave passed off, only Henery White spoke up for 'im, and said that he scarcely ever 'ad a pint but wot somebody else paid for it. There was unpleasantness all round then, and in the row somebody knocked one o' Henery's teeth out.

"And that wasn't the only unpleasantness, and at last some of the chaps put their 'eads together and agreed among theirselves to try and help Job Brown to give up the drink. They kep' it secret from Job, but the next time 'e came in and ordered a pint Joe Gubbins—'aving won the toss—drank it by mistake, and went straight off 'ome as 'ard as 'e could, smacking 'is lips.

"He 'ad the best of it, the other chaps 'aving to 'old Job down in 'is chair, and trying their 'ardest to explain that Joe Gubbins was only doing him a kindness. He seemed to understand at last, and arter a long time 'e said as 'e could see Joe meant to do 'im a kindness, but 'e'd better not do any more.

"He kept a very tight 'old o' the next pint, and as 'e set down at the table he looked round nasty like and asked 'em whether there was any more as would like to do 'im a kindness, and Henery White said there was, and he went straight off 'ome arter fust dropping a handful o' sawdust into Job's mug.

"I'm an old man, an' I've seen a good many rows in my time, but I've never seen anything like the one that 'appened then. It was no good talking to Job, not a bit, he being that unreasonable that even when 'is own words was repeated to 'im he wouldn't listen. He behaved like a madman, an' the langwidge 'e used was that fearful and that wicked that Smith the landlord said 'e wouldn't 'ave it in 'is house.

"Arter that you'd ha' thought that Job Brown would 'ave left off 'is talk about being teetotaler, but he didn't. He said they was quite right in trying to do 'im a kindness, but he didn't like the way they did it. He said there was a right way and a wrong way of doing everything, and they'd chose the wrong.

"It was all very well for 'im to talk, but the chaps said 'e might drink hisself to death for all they cared. And instead of seeing 'im safe 'ome as they used to when 'e was worse than usual he 'ad to look arter hisself and get 'ome as best he could.

"It was through that at last 'e came to offer five pounds reward to anybody as could 'elp 'im to become a teetotaler. He went off 'ome one night as usual, and arter stopping a few seconds in the parlour to pull hisself together, crept quietly upstairs for fear of waking 'is wife. He saw by the crack under the door that she'd left a candle burning, so he pulled hisself together agin and then turned the 'andle and went in and began to try an' take off 'is coat.

"He 'appened to give a 'alf-look towards the bed as 'e did so, and then 'e started back and rubbed 'is eyes and told 'imself he'd be better in a minute. Then 'e looked agin, for 'is wife was nowhere to be seen, and in the bed all fast and sound asleep and snoring their 'ardest was little Dick Weed the tailor and Mrs. Weed and the baby.

"Job Brown rubbed 'is eyes again, and then 'e drew hisself up to 'is full height, and putting one 'and on the chest o' drawers to steady hisself stood there staring at 'em and getting madder and madder every second. Then 'e gave a nasty cough, and Dick and Mrs. Weed an' the baby all woke up and stared at 'im as though they could 'ardly believe their eyesight.

"'Wot do you want?' ses Dick Weed, starting up.

"'Get up,' ses Job, 'ardly able to speak. I'm surprised at you. Get up out o' my bed direckly.'

"'Your bed?' screams little Dick; 'you're the worse for licker, Job Brown. Can't you see you've come into the wrong house?'

"'Eh?' ses Job, staring. 'Wrong 'ouse? Well, where's mine, then?'

"'Next door but one, same as it always was,' ses Dick. 'Will you go?'

"'A' right,' ses Job, staring. 'Well, goo'-night, Dick. Goo'-night, Mrs. Weed. Goo'-night, baby.'

"'Good-night,' ses Mrs. Weed from under the bedclothes.

"'Goo'-night, baby,' ses Job, again.

"'It can't talk yet,' ses Dick. 'Will you go?

"'Can't talk—why not?' ses Job.

"Dick didn't answer 'im.

"'Well, goo'-night, Dick,' he ses agin.

"'Good-night,' ses Dick from between 'is teeth.

"'Goo'-night, Mrs. Weed,' ses Job.

"Mrs. Weed forced herself to say 'good-night' agin.

"'Goo'-night, baby,' ses Job.

"'Look 'ere,' ses Dick, raving, 'are you goin' to stay 'ere all night, Job Brown?'

"Job didn't answer 'im, but began to go downstairs, saying 'goo'-night' as 'e went, and he'd got pretty near to the bottom when he suddenly wondered wot 'e was going downstairs for instead of up, and lading gently at 'is foolishness for making sich a mistake 'e went upstairs agin. His surprise when 'e see Dick Weed and Mrs. Weed and the baby all in 'is bed pretty near took 'is breath away.

"'Wot are you doing in my bed?' he ses.

"'It's our bed,' ses Dick, trembling all over with rage. 'I've told you afore you've come into the wrong 'ouse.'

"'Wrong 'ouse,' ses Job, staring round the room. 'I b'leeve you're right. Goo'-night, Dick; goo'-night, Mrs. Weed; goo'-night, baby.'

"Dick jumped out of bed then and tried to push 'im out of the room, but 'e was a very small man, and Job just stood there and wondered wot he was doing. Mrs. Weed and the baby both started screaming one against the other, and at last Dick pushed the window open and called out for help.

"They 'ad the neighbours in then, and the trouble they 'ad to get Job downstairs wouldn't be believed. Mrs. Pottle went for 'is wife at last, and then Job went 'ome with 'er like a lamb, asking 'er where she'd been all the evening, and saying 'e'd been looking for 'er everywhere.

"There was such a to-do about it in the village next morning that Job Brown was fairly scared. All the wimmen was out at their doors talking about it, and saying wot a shame it was and 'ow silly Mrs. Weed was to put up with it. Then old Mrs. Gumm, 'er grandmother, who was eighty-eight years old, stood outside Job's 'ouse nearly all day, shaking 'er stick at 'im and daring of 'im to come out. Wot with Mrs. Gumm and the little crowd watching 'er all day and giving 'er good advice, which she wouldn't take, Job was afraid to show 'is nose outside the door.

"He wasn't like hisself that night up at the Cauliflower. 'E sat up in the corner and wouldn't take any notice of anybody, and it was easy to see as he was thoroughly ashamed of hisself.

"'Cheer up, Job,' says Bill Chambers, at last; 'you ain't the fust man as has made a fool of hisself.'

"'Mind your own business,' ses Job Brown, 'and I'll mind mine.'

"'Why don't you leave 'im alone, Bill?' ses Henery White; 'you can see the man is worried because the baby can't talk.'

"'Oh,' ses Bill, 'I thought 'e was worried because 'is wife could.'

"All the chaps, except Job, that is, laughed at that; but Job 'e got up and punched the table, and asked whether there was anybody as would like to go outside with him for five minutes. Then 'e sat down agin, and said 'ard things agin the drink, which 'ad made 'im the larfing-stock of all the fools in Claybury.

"'I'm going to give it up, Smith,' he ses.

"'Yes, I know you are,' ses Smith.

"'If I could on'y lose the taste of it for a time I could give it up,' ses Job, wiping 'is mouth, 'and to prove I'm in earnest I'll give five pounds to anybody as'll prevent me tasting intoxicating licker for a month.'

"'You may as well save your breath to bid people "good-night" with, Job,' ses Bill Chambers; 'you wouldn't pay up if anybody did keep you off it.'

"Job swore honour bright he would, but nobody believed 'im, and at last he called for pen and ink and wrote it all down on a sheet o' paper and signed it, and then he got two other chaps to sign it as witnesses.

"Bill Chambers wasn't satisfied then. He pointed out that earning the five pounds, and then getting it out o' Job Brown arterwards, was two such entirely different things that there was no likeness between 'em at all. Then Job Brown got so mad 'e didn't know wot 'e was doing, and 'e 'anded over five pounds to Smith the landlord and wrote on the paper that he was to give it to anybody who should earn it, without consulting 'im at all. Even Bill couldn't think of anything to say agin that, but he made a point of biting all the sovereigns.

"There was quite a excitement for a few days. Henery White 'e got a 'eadache with thinking, and Joe Gubbins, 'e got a 'eadache for drinking Job Brown's beer agin. There was all sorts o' wild ways mentioned to earn that five pounds, but they didn't come to anything.

"Arter a week had gone by Job Brown began to get restless like, and once or twice 'e said in Smith's hearing 'ow useful five pounds would be. Smith didn't take any notice, and at last Job told 'im there didn't seem any likelihood of the five pounds being earned, and he wanted it to buy pigs with. The way 'e went on when Smith said 'e 'adn't got the power to give it back, and 'e'd got to keep it in trust for anybody as might earn it, was disgraceful.

"He used to ask Smith for it every night, and Smith used to give 'im the same answer, until at last Job Brown said he'd go an' see a lawyer about it. That frightened Smith a bit, and I b'lieve he'd ha' 'anded it over, but two days arterwards Job was going upstairs so careful that he fell down to the bottom and broke 'is leg.

"It was broken in two places, and the doctor said it would be a long job, owing to 'is drinking habits, and 'e gave Mrs. Brown strict orders that Job wasn't to 'ave a drop of anything, even if 'e asked for it.

"There was a lot o' talk about it up at the Cauliflower 'ere, and Henery White, arter a bad 'eadache, thought of a plan by which 'e and Bill Chambers could 'ave that five pounds atween 'em. The idea was that Bill Chambers was to go with Henery to see Job, and take 'im a bottle of beer, and jist as Job was going to drink it Henery should knock it out of 'is 'ands, at the same time telling Bill Chambers 'e ought to be ashamed o' hisself.

"It was a good idea, and, as Henery White said, if Mrs. Brown was in the room so much the better, as she'd be a witness. He made Bill swear to keep it secret for fear of other chaps doing it arterwards, and then they bought a bottle o' beer and set off up the road to Job's. The annoying part of it was, arter all their trouble and Henery White's 'eadache, Mrs. Brown wouldn't let 'em in. They begged and prayed of 'er to let 'em go up and just 'ave a peep at 'im, but she wouldn't She said she'd go upstairs and peep for 'em, and she came down agin and said that 'e was a little bit flushed, but sleeping like a lamb.

"They went round the corner and drank the ale up, and Bill Chambers said it was a good job. Henery thought 'e was clever, because nobody else did. As for 'is 'eadaches, he put 'em down to over-eating.

"Several other chaps called to see Job, but none of them was allowed to go up, and for seven weeks that unfortunate man never touched a drop of anything. The doctor tried to persuade 'im now that 'e 'ad got the start to keep it, and 'e likewise pointed out that as 'e had been without liquor for over a month, he could go and get that five pounds back out o' Smith.

"Job promised that 'e would give it up; but the fust day 'e felt able to crawl on 'is crutches he made up 'is mind to go up to the Cauliflower and see whether gin and beer tasted as good as it used to. The only thing was 'is wife might stop 'im.

"'You're done up with nursing me, old gal,' he ses to 'is wife.

"'I am a bit tired,' ses she.

"'I could see it by your eyes,' ses Job. 'What you want is a change, Polly. Why not go and see your sister at Wickham?"

"'I don't like leaving you alone,' ses Mrs. Brown, 'else I'd like to go. I want to do a little shopping.'

"'You go, my dear,' ses Job. 'I shall be quite 'appy sitting at the gate in the sun with a glass o' milk an' a pipe.'

"He persuaded 'er at last, and, in a fit o' generosity, gave 'er three shillings to go shopping with, and as soon as she was out o' sight he went off with a crutch and a stick, smiling all over 'is face. He met Dick Weed in the road and they shook 'ands quite friendly, and Job asked 'im to 'ave a drink. Then Henery White and some more chaps came along, and by the time they got to the Cauliflower they was as merry a party as you'd wish to see.

"Every man 'ad a pint o' beer, which Job paid for, not forgetting Smith 'isself, and Job closed 'is eyes with pleasure as 'e took his. Then they began to talk about 'is accident, and Job showed 'em is leg and described wot it felt like to be a teetotaler for seven weeks.

"'And I'll trouble you for that five pounds, Smith,' 'e ses, smiling. 'I've been without anything stronger than milk for seven weeks. I never thought when I wrote that paper I was going to earn my own money.'

"'None of us did, Job,' ses Smith. 'D'ye think that leg'll be all right agin? As good as the other, I mean?'

"'Doctor ses so,' ses Job.

"'It's wonderful wot they can do nowadays,' ses Smith, shaking 'is 'ead.

"''Strordinary,' ses Job; 'where's that five pounds, Smith?'

"'You don't want to put any sudden weight or anything like that on it for a time, Job,' ses Smith; 'don't get struggling or fighting, whatever you do, Job.'

"''Taint so likely,' ses Job; 'd'ye think I'm a fool? Where's that five pounds, Smith?'

"'Ah, yes,' ses Smith, looking as though 'e'd just remembered something. 'I wanted to tell you about that, to see if I've done right. I'm glad you've come in.'

"'Eh?' ses Job Brown, staring at 'im.

"'Has your wife gone shopping to-day?' ses Smith, looking at 'im very solemn.

"Job Brown put 'is mug down on the table and turned as pale as ashes. Then 'e got up and limped over to the bar.

"'Wot d'yer mean' he ses, choking.

"'She said she thought o' doing so,' ses Smith, wiping a glass; 'she came in yesterday and asked for that five pounds she'd won. The doctor came in with 'er and said she'd kept you from licker for seven weeks, let alone a month; so, according to the paper, I 'ad to give it to 'er. I 'ope I done right, Job?'

"Job didn't answer 'im a word, good or bad. He just turned 'is back on him, and, picking up 'is crutch and 'is stick, hobbled off 'ome. Henery White tried to make 'im stop and 'ave another pint, but he wouldn't. He said he didn't want 'is wife to find 'im out when she returned."

"THE TOLL-HOUSE"

"It's all nonsense," said Jack Barnes. "Of course people have died in the house; people die in every house. As for the noises—wind in the chimney and rats in the wainscot are very convincing to a nervous man. Give me another cup of tea, Meagle."

"Lester and White are first," said Meagle, who was presiding at the tea-table of the Three Feathers Inn. "You've had two."

Lester and White finished their cups with irritating slowness, pausing between sips to sniff the aroma, and to discover the sex and dates of arrival of the "strangers" which floated in some numbers in the beverage. Mr. Meagle served them to the brim, and then, turning to the grimly expectant Mr. Barnes, blandly requested him to ring for hot water.

"We'll try and keep your nerves in their present healthy condition," he remarked. "For my part I have a sort of half-and-half belief in the super-natural."

"All sensible people have," said Lester. "An aunt of mine saw a ghost once."

White nodded.

"I had an uncle that saw one," he said.

"It always is somebody else that sees them," said Barnes.

"Well, there is a house," said Meagle, "a large house at an absurdly low rent, and nobody will take it. It has taken toll of at least one life of every family that has lived there—however short the time— and since it has stood empty caretaker after care-taker has died there. The last caretaker died fifteen years ago."

"Exactly," said Barnes. "Long enough ago for legends to accumulate."

"I'll bet you a sovereign you won't spend the night there alone, for all your talk," said White, suddenly.

"And I," said Lester.

"No," said Barnes slowly. "I don't believe in ghosts nor in any supernatural things whatever; all the same I admit that I should not care to pass a night there alone."

"But why not?" inquired White.

"Wind in the chimney," said Meagle with a grin.

"Rats in the wainscot," chimed in Lester. "As you like," said Barnes coloring.

"Suppose we all go," said Meagle. "Start after supper, and get there about eleven. We have been walking for ten days now without an adventure—except Barnes's discovery that ditchwater smells longest. It will be a novelty, at any rate, and, if we break the spell by all surviving, the grateful owner ought to come down handsome."

"Let's see what the landlord has to say about it first," said Lester. "There is no fun in passing a night in an ordinary empty house. Let us make sure that it is haunted."

He rang the bell, and, sending for the landlord, appealed to him in the name of our common humanity not to let them waste a night watching in a house in which spectres and hobgoblins had no part. The reply was more than reassuring, and the landlord, after describing with considerable art the exact appearance of a head which had been seen hanging out of a window in the moonlight, wound up with a polite but urgent request that they would settle his bill before they went.

"It's all very well for you young gentlemen to have your fun," he said indulgently; "but supposing as how you are all found dead in the morning, what about me? It ain't called the Toll-House for nothing, you know."

"Who died there last?" inquired Barnes, with an air of polite derision.

"A tramp," was the reply. "He went there for the sake of half a crown, and they found him next morning hanging from the balusters, dead."

"Suicide," said Barnes. "Unsound mind."

The landlord nodded. "That's what the jury brought it in," he said slowly; "but his mind was sound enough when he went in there. I'd known him, off and on, for years. I'm a poor man, but I wouldn't spend the night in that house for a hundred pounds."

He repeated this remark as they started on their expedition a few hours later. They left as the inn was closing for the night; bolts shot noisily behind them, and, as the regular customers trudged slowly homewards, they set off at a brisk pace in the direction of the house. Most of the cottages were already in darkness, and lights in others went out as they passed.

"It seems rather hard that we have got to lose a night's rest in order to convince Barnes of the existence of ghosts," said White.

"It's in a good cause," said Meagle. "A most worthy object; and something seems to tell me that we shall succeed. You didn't forget the candles, Lester?"

"I have brought two," was the reply; "all the old man could spare."

There was but little moon, and the night was cloudy. The road between high hedges was dark, and in one place, where it ran through a wood, so black that they twice stumbled in the uneven ground at the side of it.

"Fancy leaving our comfortable beds for this!" said White again. "Let me see; this desirable residential sepulchre lies to the right, doesn't it?"

"Farther on," said Meagle.

They walked on for some time in silence, broken only by White's tribute to the softness, the cleanliness, and the comfort of the bed which was receding farther and farther into the distance. Under Meagle's guidance they turned oft at last to the right, and, after a walk of a quarter of a mile, saw the gates of the house before them.

The lodge was almost hidden by overgrown shrubs and the drive was choked with rank growths. Meagle leading, they pushed through it until the dark pile of the house loomed above them.

"There is a window at the back where we can get in, so the landlord says," said Lester, as they stood before the hall door.

"Window?" said Meagle. "Nonsense. Let's do the thing properly. Where's the knocker?"

He felt for it in the darkness and gave a thundering rat-tat-tat at the door.

"Don't play the fool," said Barnes crossly.

"Ghostly servants are all asleep," said Meagle gravely, "but I'll wake them up before I've done with them. It's scandalous keeping us out here in the dark."

He plied the knocker again, and the noise volleyed in the emptiness beyond. Then with a sudden exclamation he put out his hands and stumbled forward.

"Why, it was open all the time," he said, with an odd catch in his voice. "Come on."

"I don't believe it was open," said Lester, hanging back. "Somebody is playing us a trick."

"Nonsense," said Meagle sharply. "Give me a candle. Thanks. Who's got a match?"

Barnes produced a box and struck one, and Meagle, shielding the candle with his hand, led the way forward to the foot of the stairs. "Shut the door, somebody," he said, "there's too much draught."

"It is shut," said White, glancing behind him.

Meagle fingered his chin. "Who shut it?" he inquired, looking from one to the other. "Who came in last?"

"I did," said Lester, "but I don't remember shutting it—perhaps I did, though."

Meagle, about to speak, thought better of it, and, still carefully guarding the flame, began to explore the house, with the others close behind. Shadows danced on the walls and lurked in the corners as they proceeded. At the end of the passage they found a second staircase, and ascending it slowly gained the first floor.

"Careful!" said Meagle, as they gained the landing.

He held the candle forward and showed where the balusters had broken away. Then he peered curiously into the void beneath.

"This is where the tramp hanged himself, I suppose," he said thoughtfully.

"You've got an unwholesome mind," said White, as they walked on. "This place is qutie creepy enough without your remembering that. Now let's find a comfortable room and have a little nip of whiskey apiece and a pipe. How will this do?"

He opened a door at the end of the passage and revealed a small square room. Meagle led the way with the candle, and, first melting a drop or two of tallow, stuck it on the mantelpiece. The others seated themselves on the floor and watched pleasantly as White drew from his pocket a small bottle of whiskey and a tin cup.

"H'm! I've forgotten the water," he exclaimed. "I'll soon get some," said Meagle.

He tugged violently at the bell-handle, and the rusty jangling of a bell sounded from a distant kitchen. He rang again.

"Don't play the fool," said Barnes roughly.

Meagle laughed. "I only wanted to convince you," he said kindly. "There ought to be, at any rate, one ghost in the servants' hall."

Barnes held up his hand for silence.

"Yes?" said Meagle with a grin at the other two. "Is anybody coming?"

"Suppose we drop this game and go back," said Barnes suddenly. "I don't believe in spirits, but nerves are outside anybody's command. You may laugh as you like, but it really seemed to me that I heard a door open below and steps on the stairs."

His voice was drowned in a roar of laughter.

"He is coming round," said Meagle with a smirk. "By the time I have done with him he will be a confirmed believer. Well, who will go and get some water? Will you, Barnes?"

"No," was the reply.

"If there is any it might not be safe to drink after all these years," said Lester. "We must do without it."

Meagle nodded, and taking a seat on the floor held out his hand for the cup. Pipes were lit and the clean, wholesome smell of tobacco filled the room. White produced a pack of cards; talk and laughter rang through the room and died away reluctantly in distant corridors.

"Empty rooms always delude me into the belief that I possess a deep voice," said Meagle. "To-morrow—"

He started up with a smothered exclamation as the light went out suddenly and something struck him on the head. The others sprang to their feet. Then Meagle laughed.

"It's the candle," he exclaimed. "I didn't stick it enough."

Barnes struck a match and relighting the candle stuck it on the mantelpiece, and sitting down took up his cards again.

"What was I going to say?" said Meagle. "Oh, I know; to-morrow I—"

"Listen!" said White, laying his hand on the other's sleeve. "Upon my word I really thought I heard a laugh."

"Look here!" said Barnes. "What do you say to going back? I've had enough of this. I keep fancying that I hear things too; sounds of something moving about in the passage outside. I know it's only fancy, but it's uncomfortable."

"You go if you want to," said Meagle, "and we will play dummy. Or you might ask the tramp to take your hand for you, as you go downstairs."

Barnes shivered and exclaimed angrily. He got up and, walking to the half-closed door, listened.

"Go outside," said Meagle, winking at the other two. "I'll dare you to go down to the hall door and back by yourself."

Barnes came back and, bending forward, lit his pipe at the candle.

"I am nervous but rational," he said, blowing out a thin cloud of smoke. "My nerves tell me that there is something prowling up and down the long passage outside; my reason tells me that it is all nonsense. Where are my cards?"

He sat down again, and taking up his hand, looked through it carefully and led.

"Your play, White," he said after a pause. White made no sign.

"Why, he is asleep," said Meagle. "Wake up, old man. Wake up and play."

Lester, who was sitting next to him, took the sleeping man by the arm and shook him, gently at first and then with some roughness; but White, with his back against the wall and his head bowed, made no sign. Meagle bawled in his ear and then turned a puzzled face to the others.

"He sleeps like the dead," he said, grimacing. "Well, there are still three of us to keep each other company."

"Yes," said Lester, nodding. "Unless—Good Lord! suppose—"

He broke off and eyed them trembling.

"Suppose what?" inquired Meagle.

"Nothing," stammered Lester. "Let's wake him. Try him again. *White! White!*"

"It's no good," said Meagle seriously; "there's something wrong about that sleep."

"That's what I meant," said Lester; "and if he goes to sleep like that, why shouldn't—"

Meagle sprang to his feet. "Nonsense," he said roughly. "He's tired out; that's all. Still, let's take him up and clear out. You take his legs and Barnes will lead the way with the candle. Yes? Who's that?"

He looked up quickly towards the door. "Thought I heard somebody tap," he said with a shamefaced laugh. "Now, Lester, up with him. One, two— Lester! Lester!"

He sprang forward too late; Lester, with his face buried in his arms, had rolled over on the floor fast asleep, and his utmost efforts failed to awaken him.

"He—is—asleep," he stammered. "'Asleep!"

Barnes, who had taken the candle from the mantel-piece, stood peering at the sleepers in silence and dropping tallow over the floor.

"We must get out of this," said Meagle. "Quick!" Barnes hesitated. "We can't leave them here—" he began.

"We must," said Meagle in strident tones. "If you go to sleep I shall go—Quick! Come."

He seized the other by the arm and strove to drag him to the door. Barnes shook him off, and putting the candle back on the mantelpiece, tried again to arouse the sleepers.

"It's no good," he said at last, and, turning from them, watched Meagle. "Don't you go to sleep," he said anxiously.

Meagle shook his head, and they stood for some time in uneasy silence. "May as well shut the door," said Barnes at last.

He crossed over and closed it gently. Then at a scuffling noise behind him he turned and saw Meagle in a heap on the hearthstone.

With a sharp catch in his breath he stood motionless. Inside the room the candle, fluttering in the draught, showed dimly the grotesque attitudes of the sleepers. Beyond the door there seemed to his over-wrought imagination a strange and stealthy unrest. He tried to whistle, but his lips were parched, and in a mechanical fashion he stooped, and began to pick up the cards which littered the floor.

He stopped once or twice and stood with bent head listening. The unrest outside seemed to increase; a loud creaking sounded from the stairs.

"Who is there?" he cried loudly.

The creaking ceased. He crossed to the door and flinging it open, strode out into the corridor. As he walked his fears left him suddenly.

"Come on!" he cried with a low laugh. "All of you! All of you! Show your faces—your infernal ugly faces! Don't skulk!"

He laughed again and walked on; and the heap in the fireplace put out his head tortoise fashion and listened in horror to the retreating footsteps. Not until they had become inaudible in the distance did the listeners' features relax.

"Good Lord, Lester, we've driven him mad," he said in a frightened whisper. "We must go after him."

There was no reply. Meagle sprung to his feet. "Do you hear?" he cried. "Stop your fooling now; this is serious. White! Lester! Do you hear?"

He bent and surveyed them in angry bewilderment. "All right," he said in a trembling voice. "You won't frighten me, you know."

He turned away and walked with exaggerated carelessness in the direction of the door. He even went outside and peeped through the crack, but the sleepers did not stir. He glanced into the blackness behind, and then came hastily into the room again.

He stood for a few seconds regarding them. The stillness in the house was horrible; he could not even hear them breathe. With a sudden resolution he snatched the candle from the mantelpiece and held the flame to White's finger. Then as he reeled back stupefied the footsteps again became audible.

He stood with the candle in his shaking hand listening. He heard them ascending the farther staircase, but they stopped suddenly as he went to the door. He walked a little way along the passage, and they went scurrying down the stairs and then at a jog-trot along the corridor below. He went back to the main staircase, and they ceased again.

For a time he hung over the balusters, listening and trying to pierce the blackness below; then slowly, step by step, he made his way downstairs, and, holding the candle above his head, peered about him.

"Barnes!" he called. "Where are you?" Shaking with fright, he made his way along the passage, and summoning up all his courage pushed open doors and gazed fearfully into empty rooms. Then, quite suddenly, he heard the footsteps in front of him.

He followed slowly for fear of extinguishing the candle, until they led him at last into a vast bare kitchen with damp walls and a broken floor. In front of him a door leading into an inside room had just closed. He ran towards it and flung it open, and a cold air blew out the candle. He stood aghast.

"Barnes!" he cried again. "Don't be afraid! It is I—Meagle!"

There was no answer. He stood gazing into the darkness, and all the time the idea of something close at hand watching was upon him. Then suddenly the steps broke out overhead again.

He drew back hastily, and passing through the kitchen groped his way along the narrow passages. He could now see better in the darkness, and finding himself at last at the foot of the staircase began to ascend it noiselessly. He reached the landing just in time to see a figure disappear round the angle of a wall. Still careful to make no noise, he followed the sound of the steps until they led him to the top floor, and he cornered the chase at the end of a short passage.

"Barnes!" he whispered. "Barnes!"

Something stirred in the darkness. A small circular window at the end of the passage just softened the blackness and revealed the dim outlines of a motionless figure. Meagle, in place of advancing, stood almost as still as a sudden horrible doubt took possession of him. With his eyes fixed on the shape in front he fell back slowly and, as it advanced upon him, burst into a terrible cry.

"Barnes! For God's sake! Is it you?"

The echoes of his voice left the air quivering, but the figure before him paid no heed. For a moment he tried to brace his courage up to endure its approach, then with a smothered cry he turned and fled.

The passages wound like a maze, and he threaded them blindly in a vain search for the stairs. If he could get down and open the hall door—

He caught his breath in a sob; the steps had begun again. At a lumbering trot they clattered up and down the bare passages, in and out, up and down, as though in search of him. He stood appalled, and then as they drew near entered a small room and stood behind the door as they rushed by. He came out and ran swiftly and noiselessly in the other direction, and in a moment the steps were after him. He found the long corridor and raced along it at top speed. The stairs he knew were at the end, and with the steps close behind he descended them in blind haste. The steps gained on him, and he shrank to the side to let them pass, still continuing his headlong flight. Then suddenly he seemed to slip off the earth into space.

Lester awoke in the morning to find the sunshine streaming into the room, and White sitting up and regarding with some perplexity a badly blistered finger.

"Where are the others?" inquired Lester. "Gone, I suppose," said White. "We must have been asleep."

Lester arose, and stretching his stiffened limbs, dusted his clothes with his hands, and went out into the corridor. White followed. At the noise of their approach a figure which had been lying asleep at the other end sat up and revealed the face of Barnes. "Why, I've been asleep," he said in surprise. "I don't remember coming here. How did I get here?"

"Nice place to come for a nap," said Lester, severely, as he pointed to the gap in the balusters. "Look there! Another yard and where would you have been?"

He walked carelessly to the edge and looked over. In response to his startled cry the others drew near, and all three stood gazing at the dead man below.

The "Terrace," consisting of eight gaunt houses, faced the sea, while the back rooms commanded a view of the ancient little town some half mile distant. The beach, a waste of shingle, was desolate and bare except for a ruined bathing machine and a few pieces of linen drying in the winter sunshine. In the offing tiny steamers left a trail of smoke, while sailing-craft, their canvas glistening in the sun, slowly melted from the sight. On all these things the "Terrace" turned a stolid eye, and, counting up its gains of the previous season, wondered whether it could hold on to the next. It was a discontented "Terrace," and had become prematurely soured by a Board which refused them a pier, a band-stand, and illuminated gardens.

From the front windows of the third storey of No. 1 Mrs. Cox, gazing out to sea, sighed softly.

The season had been a bad one, and Mr. Cox had been even more troublesome than usual owing to tightness in the money market and the avowed preference of local publicans for cash transactions to assets in chalk and slate. In Mr. Cox's memory there never had been such a drought, and his crop of patience was nearly exhausted.

He had in his earlier days attempted to do a little work, but his health had suffered so much that his wife had become alarmed for his safety. Work invariably brought on a cough, and as he came from a family whose lungs had formed the staple conversation of their lives, he had been compelled to abandon it, and at last it came to be understood that if he would only consent to amuse himself, and not get into trouble, nothing more would be expected of him. It was not much of a life for a man of spirit, and at times it became so unbearable that Mr. Cox would disappear for days together in search of work, returning unsuccessful after many days with nerves shattered in the pursuit.

Mrs. Cox's meditations were disturbed by a knock at the front door, and, the servants having been discharged for the season, she hurried downstairs to open it, not without a hope of belated lodgers—invalids in search of an east wind. A stout, middle-aged woman in widow's weeds stood on the door-step.

"Glad to see you, my dear," said the visitor, kissing her loudly.

Mrs. Cox gave her a subdued caress in return, not from any lack of feeling, but because she did everything in a quiet and spiritless fashion.

"I've got my Uncle Joseph from London staying with us," continued the visitor, following her into the hall, "so I just got into the train and brought him down for a blow at the sea."

A question on Mrs. Cox's lips died away as a very small man who had been hidden by his niece came into sight.

"My Uncle Joseph," said Mrs. Berry; "Mr. Joseph Piper," she added.

Mr. Piper shook hands, and after a performance on the door-mat, protracted by reason of a festoon of hemp, followed his hostess into the faded drawing-room.

"And Mr. Cox?" inquired Mrs. Berry, in a cold voice.

Mrs. Cox shook her head. "He's been away this last three days," she said, flushing slightly.

"Looking for work?" suggested the visitor.

Mrs. Cox nodded, and, placing the tips of her fingers together, fidgeted gently.

"Well, I hope he finds it," said Mrs. Berry, with more venom than the remark seemed to require. "Why, where's your marble clock?"

Mrs. Cox coughed. "It's being mended," she said, confusedly.

Mrs. Berry eyed her anxiously. "Don't mind him, my dear," she said, with a jerk of her head in the direction of Mr. Piper, "he's nobody. Wouldn't you like to go out on the beach a little while, uncle?"

"No," said Mr. Piper.

"I suppose Mr. Cox took the clock for company," remarked Mrs. Berry, after a hostile stare at her relative.

Mrs. Cox sighed and shook her head. It was no use pretending with Mrs. Berry.

"He'll pawn the clock and anything else he can lay his hands on, and when he's drunk it up come home to be made a fuss of," continued Mrs. Berry, heatedly; "that's you men."

Her glance was so fiery that Mr. Joseph Piper was unable to allow the remark to pass unchallenged.

"I never pawned a clock," he said, stroking his little grey head.

"That's a lot to boast of, isn't it?" demanded his niece; "if I hadn't got anything better than that to boast of I wouldn't boast at all."

Mr. Piper said that he was not boasting.

"It'll go on like this, my dear, till you're ruined," said the sympathetic Mrs. Berry, turning to her friend again; "what'll you do then?"

"Yes, I know," said Mrs. Cox. "I've had a bad season, too, and I'm so anxious about him in spite of it all. I can't sleep at nights for fearing that he's in some trouble. I'm sure I laid awake half last night crying."

Mrs. Berry sniffed loudly, and Mr. Piper making a remark in a low voice, turned on him with ferocity.

"What did you say?" she demanded.

"I said it does her credit," said Mr. Piper, firmly.

"I might have known it was nonsense," retorted his niece, hotly. "Can't you get him to take the pledge, Mary?"

"I couldn't insult him like that," said Mrs. Cox, with a shiver; "you don't know his pride. He never admits that he drinks; he says that he only takes a little for his indigestion. He'd never forgive me. When he pawns the things he pretends that somebody has stolen them, and the way he goes on at me for my carelessness is alarming. He gets worked up to such a pitch that sometimes I almost think he believes it himself."

"Rubbish," said Mrs. Berry, tartly, "you're too easy with him."

Mrs. Cox sighed, and, leaving the room, returned with a bottle of wine which was port to the look and red-currant to the taste, and a seedcake of formidable appearance. The visitors attacked these refreshments mildly, Mr. Piper sipping his wine with an obtrusive carefulness which his niece rightly regarded as a reflection upon her friend's hospitality.

"What Cox wants is a shock," she said; "you've dropped some crumbs on the carpet, uncle."

Mr. Piper apologised and said he had got his eye on them, and would pick them up when he had finished and pick up his niece's at the same time to prevent her stooping. Mrs. Berry, in an aside to Mrs. Cox, said that her Uncle Joseph's tongue had got itself disliked on both sides of the family.

"And I'd give him one," said Mrs. Berry, returning again to the subject of Mr. Cox and shocks. "He has a gentleman's life of it here, and he would look rather silly if you were sold up and he had to do something for his living."

"It's putting away the things that is so bad," said Mrs. Cox, shaking her head; "that clock won't last him out, I know; he'll come back and take some of the other things. Every spring I have to go through his pockets for the tickets and get the things out again, and I mustn't say a word for fear of hurting his feelings. If I do he goes off again."

"If I were you," said Mrs. Berry, emphatically, "I'd get behind with the rent or something and have the brokers in. He'd look rather astonished if he came home and saw a broker's man sitting in a chair—"

"He'd look more astonished if he saw him sitting in a flower-pot," suggested the caustic Mr. Piper.

"I couldn't do that," said Mrs. Cox. "I couldn't stand the disgrace, even though I knew I could pay him out. As it is, Cox is always setting his family above mine."

Mrs. Berry, without ceasing to stare Mr. Piper out of countenance, shook her head, and, folding her arms, again stated her opinion that Mr. Cox wanted a shock, and expressed a great yearning to be the humble means of giving him one.

"If you can't have the brokers in, get somebody to pretend to be one," she said, sharply; "that would prevent him pawning any more things, at any rate. Why wouldn't he do?" she added, nodding at her uncle.

Anxiety on Mrs. Cox's face was exaggerated on that of Mr. Piper.

"Let uncle pretend to be a broker's man in for the rent," continued the excitable lady, rapidly. "When Mr. Cox turns up after his spree, tell him what his doings have brought you to, and say you'll have to go to the workhouse."

"I look like a broker's man, don't I?" said Mr. Piper, in a voice more than tinged with sarcasm.

"Yes," said his niece, "that's what put it into my head."

"It's very kind of you, dear, and very kind of Mr. Piper," said Mrs. Cox, "but I couldn't think of it, I really couldn't."

"Uncle would be delighted," said Mrs. Berry, with a wilful blinking of plain facts. "He's got nothing better to do; it's a nice house and good food, and he could sit at the open window and sniff at the sea all day long."

Mr. Piper sniffed even as she spoke, but not at the sea.

"And I'll come for him the day after to-morrow," said Mrs. Berry.

It was the old story of the stronger will: Mrs. Cox after a feeble stand gave way altogether, and Mr. Piper's objections were demolished before he had given them full utterance. Mrs. Berry went off alone after dinner, secretly glad to have got rid of Mr. Piper, who was making a self-invited stay at her house of indefinite duration; and Mr. Piper, in his new rôle of broker's man, essayed the part with as much help as a clay pipe and a pint of beer could afford him.

That day and the following he spent amid the faded grandeurs of the drawing-room, gazing longingly at the wide expanse of beach and the tumbling sea beyond. The house was almost uncannily quiet, an occasional tinkle of metal or crash of china from the basement giving the only indication of the industrious Mrs. Cox; but on the day after the quiet of the house was broken by the return of its master, whose annoyance, when he found the drawing-room clock stolen and a man in possession, was alarming in its vehemence. He lectured his wife severely on her mismanagement, and after some hesitation announced his intention of going through her books. Mrs. Cox gave them to him, and, armed with pen and ink and four square inches of pink blotting-paper, he performed feats of balancing which made him a very Blondin of finance.

"I shall have to get something to do," he said, gloomily, laying down his pen.

"Yes, dear," said his wife.

Mr. Cox leaned back in his chair and, wiping his pen on the blotting-paper, gazed in a speculative fashion round the room. "Have you any money?" he inquired.

For reply his wife rummaged in her pocket and after a lengthy search produced a bunch of keys, a thimble, a needle-case, two pocket-handkerchiefs, and a halfpenny. She put this last on the table, and Mr. Cox, whose temper had been mounting steadily, threw it to the other end of the room.

"I can't help it," said Mrs. Cox, wiping her eyes. "I'm sure I've done all I could to keep a home together. I can't even raise money on anything."

Mr. Cox, who had been glancing round the room again, looked up sharply.

"Why not?" he inquired.

"The broker's man," said Mrs. Cox, nervously; "he's made an inventory of everything, and he holds us responsible."

Mr. Cox leaned back in his chair. "This is a pretty state of things," he blurted, wildly. "Here have I been walking my legs off looking for work, any work so long as it's honest labour, and I come back to find a broker's man sitting in my own house and drinking up my beer."

He rose and walked up and down the room, and Mrs. Cox, whose nerves were hardly equal to the occasion, slipped on her bonnet and announced her intention of trying to obtain a few necessaries on credit. Her husband waited in indignant silence until he heard the front door close behind her, and then stole softly upstairs to have a look at the fell destroyer of his domestic happiness.

Mr. Piper, who was already very tired of his imprisonment, looked up curiously as he heard the door pushed open, and discovered an elderly gentleman with an appearance of great stateliness staring at him. In the ordinary way he was one of the meekest of men, but the insolence of this stare was outrageous. Mr. Piper, opening his mild blue eyes wide, stared back. Whereupon Mr. Cox, fumbling in his vest pocket, found a pair of folders, and putting them astride his nose, gazed at the pseudo-broker's man with crushing effect.

"What do you want here?" he asked, at length. "Are you the father of one of the servants?"

"I'm the father of all the servants in the house," said Mr. Piper, sweetly.

"Don't answer me, sir," said Mr. Cox, with much pomposity; "you're an eyesore to an honest man, a vulture, a harpy."

Mr. Piper pondered.

"How do you know what's an eyesore to an honest man?" he asked, at length.

Mr. Cox smiled scornfully.

"Where is your warrant or order, or whatever you call it?" he demanded.

"I've shown it to Mrs. Cox," said Mr. Piper.

"Show it to me," said the other.

"I've complied with the law by showing it once," said Mr. Piper, bluffing, "and I'm not going to show it again."

Mr. Cox stared at him disdainfully, beginning at his little sleek grey head and travelling slowly downwards to his untidy boots and then back again. He repeated this several times, until Mr. Piper, unable to bear it patiently, began to eye him in the same fashion.

"What are you looking at, vulture?" demanded the incensed Mr. Cox.

"Three spots o' grease on a dirty weskit," replied Mr. Piper, readily, "a pair o' bow legs in a pair o' somebody else's trousers, and a shabby coat wore under the right arm, with carrying off"—he paused a moment as though to make sure—"with carrying off of a drawing-room clock."

He regretted this retort almost before he had finished it, and rose to his feet with a faint cry of alarm as the heated Mr. Cox first locked the door and put the key in his pocket and then threw up the window.

"Vulture!" he cried, in a terrible voice.

"Yes, sir," said the trembling Mr. Piper.

Mr. Cox waved his hand towards the window.

"Fly," he said, briefly.

Mr. Piper tried to form his white lips into a smile, and his knees trembled beneath him.

"Did you hear what I said?" demanded Mr. Cox. "What are you waiting for? If you don't fly out of the window I'll throw you out."

"Don't touch me," screamed Mr. Piper, retreating behind a table, "it's all a mistake. All a joke. I'm not a broker's man. Ha! ha!"

"Eh?" said the other; "not a broker's man? What are you, then?"

In eager, trembling tones Mr. Piper told him, and, gathering confidence as he proceeded, related the conversation which had led up to his imposture. Mr. Cox listened in a dazed fashion, and as he concluded threw himself into a chair, and gave way to a terrible outburst of grief.

"The way I've worked for that woman," he said, brokenly, "to think it should come to this! The deceit of the thing; the wickedness of it My heart is broken; I shall never be the same man again—never!"

Mr. Piper made a sympathetic noise.

"It's been very unpleasant for me," he said, "but my niece is so masterful."

"I don't blame you," said Mr. Cox, kindly; "shake hands."

They shook hands solemnly, and Mr. Piper, muttering something about a draught, closed the window.

"You might have been killed in trying to jump out of that window," said Mr. Cox; "fancy the feelings of those two deceitful women then."

"Fancy my feelings!" said Mr. Piper, with a shudder. "Playing with fire, that's what I call it. My niece is coming this afternoon; it would serve her right if you gave her a fright by telling her you had killed me. Perhaps it would be a lesson to her not to be so officious."

"It would serve 'em both right," agreed Mr. Cox; "only Mrs. Berry might send for the police."

"I never thought of that," said Mr. Piper, fondling his chin.

"I might frighten my wife," mused the amiable Mr. Cox; "it would be a lesson to her not to be deceitful again. And, by Jove, I'll get some money from her to escape with; I know she's got some, and if she hasn't she will have in a day or two. There's a little pub at Newstead, eight miles from here, where we could be as happy as fighting cocks with a fiver or two. And while we're there enjoying ourselves my wife'll be half out of her mind trying to account for your disappearance to Mrs. Berry."

"It sounds all right," said Mr. Piper, cautiously, "but she won't believe you. You don't look wild enough to have killed anybody."

"I'll look wild enough when the time comes," said the other, nodding. "You get on to the White Horse at Newstead and wait for me. I'll let you out at the back way. Come along."

"But you said it was eight miles," said Mr. Piper.

"Eight miles easy walking," rejoined Mr. Cox. "Or there's a train at three o'clock. There's a sign-post at the corner there, and if you don't hurry I shall be able to catch you up. Good-bye."

He patted the hesitating Mr. Piper on the back, and letting him out through the garden, indicated the road. Then he returned to the drawing-room, and carefully rumpling his hair, tore his collar from the stud, overturned a couple of chairs and a small table, and sat down to wait as patiently as he could for the return of his wife.

He waited about twenty minutes, and then he heard a key turn in the door below and his wife's footsteps slowly mounting the stairs. By the time she reached the drawing-room his tableau was complete, and she fell back with a faint shriek at the frenzied figure which met her eyes.

"Hush," said the tragedian, putting his finger to his lips.

"Henry, what is it?" cried Mrs. Cox. "What is the matter?"

"The broker's man," said her husband, in a thrilling whisper. "We had words—he struck me. In a fit of fury I—I—choked him."

"Much?" inquired the bewildered woman.

"Much?" repeated Mr. Cox, frantically. "I've killed him and hidden the body. Now I must escape and fly the country."

The bewilderment on Mrs. Cox's face increased; she was trying to reconcile her husband's statement with a vision of a trim little figure which she had seen ten minutes before with its head tilted backwards studying the sign-post, and which she was now quite certain was Mr. Piper.

"Are you sure he's dead?" she inquired.

"Dead as a door nail," replied Mr. Cox, promptly. "I'd no idea he was such a delicate little man. What am I to do? Every moment adds to my danger. I must fly. How much money have you got?"

The question explained everything. Mrs. Cox closed her lips with a snap and shook her head.

"Don't play the fool," said her husband, wildly; "my neck's in danger."

"I haven't got anything," asseverated Mrs. Cox. "It's no good looking like that, Henry, I can't make money."

Mr. Cox's reply was interrupted by a loud knock at the hall door, which he was pleased to associate with the police. It gave him a fine opportunity for melodrama, in the midst of which his wife, rightly guessing that Mrs. Berry had returned according to arrangement, went to the door to admit her. The visitor was only busy two minutes on the door-mat, but in that time Mrs. Cox was able in low whispers to apprise her of the state of affairs.

"That's my uncle all over," said Mrs. Berry, fiercely; "that's just the mean trick I should have expected of him. You leave 'em to me, my dear."

She followed her friend into the drawing-room, and having shaken hands with Mr. Cox, drew her handkerchief from her pocket and applied it to her eyes.

"She's told me all about it," she said, nodding at Mrs. Cox, "and it's worse than you think, much worse. It isn't a broker's man—it's my poor uncle, Joseph Piper."

"Your uncle!" repeated Mr. Cox, reeling back; "the broker's man your uncle?"

Mrs. Berry sniffed. "It was a little joke on our part," she admitted, sinking into a chair and holding her handkerchief to her face. "Poor uncle; but I dare say he's happier where he is."

With its head tilted back, studyin Mr. Cox wiped his brow, and then, leaning his elbow on the mantelpiece, stared at her in well-simulated amazement.

"See what your joking has led to," he said, at last. "I have got to be a wanderer over the face of the earth, all on account of your jokes."

"It was an accident," murmured Mrs. Berry, "and nobody knows he was here, and I'm sure, poor dear, he hadn't got much to live for."

"It's very kind of you to look at it in that way, Susan, I'm sure," said Mrs. Cox.

"I was never one to make mischief," said Mrs. Berry. "It's no good crying over spilt milk. If uncle's killed he's killed, and there's an end of it But I don't think it's quite safe for Mr. Cox to stay here."

"Just what I say," said that gentleman, eagerly; "but I've got no money."

"You get away," said Mrs. Berry, with a warning glance at her friend, and nodding to emphasise her words; 'leave us some address to write to, and we must try and scrape twenty or thirty pounds to send you."

"Thirty?" said Mr. Cox, hardly able to believe his ears.

Mrs. Berry nodded. "You'll have to make that do to go on with," she said, pondering. "'And as soon as you get it you had better get as far away as possible before poor uncl'e is discovered. Where are we to send the money?"

Mr. Cox affected to consider.

"The White Horse, Newstead," he said at length, in a whisper; "better write it down."

Mrs. Berry obeyed; and this business being completed, Mr. Cox, after trying in vain to obtain a shilling or two cash in hand, bade them a pathetic farewell and went off down the path, for some reason best known to himself, on tiptoe.

For the first two days Messrs. Cox and Piper waited with exemplary patience for the remittance, the demands of the landlord, a man of coarse fibre, being met in the meantime by the latter gentleman from his own slender resources. They were both reasonable men, and knew from experience the difficulty of raising money at short notice; but on the fourth day, their funds being nearly exhausted, an urgent telegram was dispatched to Mrs. Cox.

Mr. Cox was alone when the reply came, and Mr. Piper, returning to the inn-parlour, was amazed and distressed at his friend's appearance.

Twice he had to address him before he seemed to be aware of his presence, and then Mr. Cox, breathing hard and staring at him strangely, handed him the message.

"Eh?" said Mr. Piper, in amaze, as he read slowly: "'No—need—send—money—Uncle—Joseph—has—come—back.—Berry,' What does it mean? Is she mad?"

Mr. Cox shook his head, and taking the paper from him, held it at arm's length and regarded it at an angle.

"How can you be there when you're supposed to be dead?" he said, at length.

"How can I be there when I'm here?" rejoined Mr. Piper, no less reasonably.

Both gentlemen lapsed into a wondering silence, devoted to the attempted solution of their own riddles. Finally Mr. Cox, seized with a bright idea that the telegram had got altered in transmission, went off to the post-office and dispatched another, which went straight to the heart of things:

"Don't—understand—is—Uncle—Joseph—alive?"

A reply was brought to the inn-parlour an hour later on. Mr. Cox opened it, gave one glance at it, and then with a suffocating cry handed it to the other. Mr. Piper took it gingerly, and his eyebrows almost disappeared as he read:

"Yes—smoking—in—drawing-room."

His first strong impression was that it was a case for the Psychical Research Society, but this romantic view faded in favour of a simple solution, propounded by Mr. Cox with much crisp-ness, that Mrs. Berry was leaving the realms of fact for those of romance. His actual words were shorter, but the meaning is the same.

"I'll go home and ask to see you," he said, fiercely; "that'll bring things to a head, I should think."

"And she'll say I've gone back to London, perhaps," said Mr. Piper, gifted with sudden clearness of vision. "You can't show her up unless you take me with you, and that'll show us up. That's her artfulness; that's Susan all over."

"She's a wicked, untruthful woman," gasped Mr. Cox.

"I never did like Susan," said Mr. Piper, with acerbity, "never."

Mr. Cox said he could easily understand it, and then, as a forlorn hope, sat down and wrote a long letter to his wife, in which, after dwelling at great length on the lamentable circumstances surrounding the sudden demise of Mr. Piper, he bade her thank Mrs. Berry for her well-meant efforts to ease his mind, and asked for the immediate dispatch of the money promised.

A reply came the following evening from Mrs. Berry herself. It was a long letter, and not only long, but badly written and crossed. It began with the weather, asked after Mr. Cox's health, and referred to the writer's; described with much minuteness a strange headache which had attacked Mrs. Cox, together with a long list of the remedies prescribed and the effects of each, and wound up in an out-of-the-way corner, in a vein of cheery optimism which reduced both readers to the verge of madness.

"Dear Uncle Joseph has quite recovered, and, in spite of a little nervousness—he was always rather timid—at meeting you again, has consented to go to the White Horse to satisfy you that he is alive. I dare say he will be with you as soon as this letter—perhaps help you to read it."

Mr. Cox laid the letter down with extreme care, and, coughing gently, glanced in a sheepish fashion at the goggle-eyed Mr. Piper.

For some time neither of them spoke. Mr. Cox was the first to break the silence and—when he had finished—Mr. Piper said "Hush."

"Besides, it does no good," he added.

"It does me good," said Mr. Cox, recommencing.

Mr. Piper held up his hand with a startled gesture for silence. The words died away on his friend's lips as a familiar voice was heard in the passage, and the next moment Mrs. Berry entered the room and stood regarding them.

"I ran down by the same train to make sure you came, uncle," she remarked. "How long have you been here?"

Mr. Piper moistened his lips and gazed wildly at Mr. Cox for guidance.

"'Bout—'bout five minutes," he stammered.

"We were so glad dear uncle wasn't hurt much," continued Mrs. Berry, smiling, and shaking her head at Mr. Cox; "but the idea of your burying him in the geranium-bed; we haven't got him clean yet."

Mr. Piper, giving utterance to uncouth noises, quitted the room hastily, but Mr. Cox sat still and stared at her dumbly.

"Weren't you surprised to see him?" inquired his tormentor.

"Not after your letter," said Mr. Cox, finding his voice at last, and speaking with an attempt at chilly dignity. "Nothing could surprise me much after that."

Mrs. Berry smiled again.

"Ah, I've got another little surprise for you," she said, briskly. "Mrs. Cox was so upset at the idea of being alone while you were a wanderer over the face of the earth, that she and I have gone into partnership. We have had a proper deed drawn up, so that now there are two of us to look after things. Eh? What did you say?"

"I was just thinking," said Mr. Cox.

TWO OF A TRADE

E's a nero, that's wot 'e is, sir," said the cook, as he emptied a boiler of dirty water overboard.

"A what?" said the skipper.

"A nero," said the cook, speaking very slowly and distinctly. "A nero in real life, a chap wot, speaking for all for'ard, we're proud to have aboard along with us."

"I didn't know he was much of a swimmer," said the skipper, glancing curiously at a clumsily-built man of middle age, who sat on the hatch glancing despondently at the side.

"No more 'e ain't," said the cook, "an' that's what makes 'im more 'eroish still in my own opinion."

"Did he take his clothes off?" inquired the mate.

"Not a bit of it," said the delighted cook; "not a pair of trowsis, nor even 'is 'at, which was sunk."

"You're a liar, cook," said the hero, looking up for a moment.

"You didn't take your trowsis off, George?" said the cook anxiously.

"I chucked my 'at on the pavement," growled George, without looking up.

"Well, anyway, you went over the Embankment after that pore girl like a Briton, didn't you?" said the other.

There was no reply.

"Didn't you?" said the cook appealingly.

"Did you expect me to go over like a Dutchman, or wot?" demanded George fiercely.

"That's 'is modesty," said the cook, turning to the others with the air of a showman. "'E can't bear us to talk about it Nearly drownded 'e was. All but, and a barge came along and shoved a boat-hook right through the seat of his trowsis an' saved 'im. Stand up an' show 'em your trowsis, George."

"If I do stand up," said George, in a voice broken with rage, "it'll be a bad day for you, my lad."

"Ain't he modest?" said the cook. "Don't it do you good to 'ear 'im? He was just like that when they got him ashore and the crowd started patting him."

"Didn't like it?" queried the mate.

"Well, they overdid it a little, p'raps," admitted the cook; "one old chap wot couldn't get near patted 'is 'ead with 'is stick, but it was all meant in the way of kindness."

"I'm proud of you, George," said the skipper heartily.

"We all are," said the mate.

George grunted.

"I'll write for the medal for him," said the skipper. "Were there any witnesses, cook?"

"Heaps of 'em," said the other, "but I gave 'em 'is name and address. 'Schooner John Henry, of Limehouse, is 'is home,' I ses, 'and George Cooper 'is name.'"

"You talked a damned sight too much," said the hero, "you lean, lop-sided son of a tinker."

"There's 'is modesty ag'in," said the cook, with a knowing smile. "'E's busting with modesty, is George. You should ha' seen 'im when a chap took 'is fortygraph."

"Took his what?" said the skipper, becoming interested.

"His fortygraph," said the cook. "'E was a young chap what was taking views for a noose-paper. 'E took George drippin' wet just as 'e come out of the water, 'e took him arter 'e 'ad 'is face wiped, an' 'e took 'im when 'e was sitting up swearing at a man wot asked 'im whether 'e was very wet."

"An' you told 'im where I lived, and what I was," said George, turning on him and shaking his fist. "You did."

"I did," said the cook simply. "You'll live to thank me for it, George."

The other gave a dreadful howl, and rising from the deck walked forward and went below, giving a brother seaman who patted his shoulder as he passed a blow in the ribs, which nearly broke them. Those on deck exchanged glances.

"Well, I don't know," said the mate, shrugging his shoulders; "seems to me if I'd saved a fellow-critter's life I shouldn't mind hearing about it."

"That's what you think," said the skipper, drawing himself up a little. "If ever you do do anything of the kind perhaps you'll feel different about it."

"Well, I don't see how you should know any more than me," said the other.

The skipper cleared his throat.

"There have been one or two little things in my life which I'm not exactly ashamed of," he said modestly.

"That ain't much to boast of," said the mate, wilfully misunderstanding him.

"I mean," said the skipper sharply, "one or two things which some people might have been proud of. But I'm proud to say that there isn't a living soul knows of 'em."

"I can quite believe that," assented the mate, and walked off with an irritating smile.

The skipper was about to follow him, to complain of the needless ambiguity of his remarks, when he was arrested by a disturbance from the foc'sle. In response to the cordial invitation of the cook, the mate and one of the hands from the brig Endeavour, moored alongside, had come aboard and gone below to look at George. The manner in which they were received was a slur upon the hospitality of the John Henry; and they came up hurriedly, declaring that they never wanted to see him again as long as they lived, and shouting offensive remarks behind them as they got over the side of their own vessel.

The skipper walked slowly to the focs'le and put his head down.

"George," he shouted.

"Sir," said the hero gruffly.

"Come down into the cabin," said the other, turning away. "I want to have a little talk with you."

George rose, and, first uttering some terrible threats against the cook, who bore them with noble fortitude, went on deck and followed the skipper to the cabin.

At his superior's request he took a seat on the locker, awkwardly enough, but smiled faintly as the skipper produced a bottle and a couple of glasses.

"Your health, George," said the skipper, as he pushed a glass towards him and raised his own.

"My bes' respec's, sir," said George, allowing the liquor to roll slowly round his mouth before swallowing it. He sighed heavily, and, putting his empty glass on the table, allowed his huge head to roll on his chest.

"Saving life don't seem to agree with you, George," said the skipper. "I like modesty, but you seem to me to carry it a trifle too far."

"It ain't modesty, sir," said George; "it's that fortygraph. When I think o' that I go 'ot all over."

"I shouldn't let that worry me if I was you, George," said the other kindly. "Looks ain't everything."

"I didn't mean it that way," said George very sourly. "My looks is good enough for me. In fact, it is partly owing to my looks, so to speak, that I'm in a mess."

"A little more rum, George?" said the skipper, whose curiosity was roused. "I don't want to know your business, far from it. But in my position as cap'n, if any of my crew gets in a mess I consider it's my duty to lend them a hand out of it, if I can."

"The world 'ud be a better place if there was more like you," said George, waxing sentimental as he sniffed delicately at the fragrant beverage. "If that noosepaper, with them pictures, gets into a certain party's 'ands, I'm ruined."

"Not if I can help it, George," said the other with great firmness. "How do you mean ruined?"

The seaman set his glass down on the little table, and, leaning over, formed a word with his lips, and then drew back slowly and watched the effect.

"What?" said the skipper.

The other repeated the performance, but beyond seeing that some word of three syllables was indicated the skipper obtained no information.

"You can speak a little louder," he said somewhat crustily.

"Bigamy!" said George, breathing the word solemnly.

"You?" said the skipper.

George nodded. "And if my first only gets hold of that paper, and sees my phiz and reads my name, I'm done for. There's my reward for saving a fellow-critter's life. Seven years."

"I'm surprised at you, George," said the skipper sternly. "Such a good wife as you've got too."

"I ain't saying nothing agin number two," grumbled George. "It's number one that didn't suit. I left her eight years ago. She was a bad 'un. I took a v'y'ge to Australia furst, just to put her out o' my mind a bit, an' I never seed her since. Where am I if she sees all about me in the paper?"

"Is she what you'd call a vindictive woman?" inquired the other. "Nasty-tempered, I mean."

"Nasty-tempered," echoed the husband of two. "If that woman could only have me put in gaol she'd stand on 'er 'ead for joy."

"Well, I'll do what I can for you if the worst comes to the worst," said the skipper. "You'd better not say anything about this to anybody else."

"Not me," said George fervently, as he rose, "an' o' course you—"

"You can rely on me," said the skipper in his most stately fashion.

He thought of the seaman's confidence several times during the evening, and, being somewhat uncertain of the law as to bigamy, sought information from the master of the Endeavour as they sat in the tetter's cabin at a quiet game of cribbage. By virtue of several appearances in the law courts with regard to collisions and spoilt cargoes this gentleman had obtained a knowledge of law which made him a recognised authority from London Bridge to the Nore.

It was a delicate matter for the master of the John Henry to broach, and, with the laudable desire of keeping the hero's secret, he approached it by a most circuitous route. He began with a burglary, followed with an attempted murder, and finally got on the subject of bigamy, via the "Deceased Wife's Sister Bill."

"What sort o' bigamy?" inquired the master of the brig.

"Oh, two wives," said Captain Thomsett.

"Yes, yes," said the other, "but are there any mitigating circumstances in the case, so that you could throw yourself on the mercy o' the court, I mean?"

"My case!" said Thomsett, glaring. "It ain't for me."

"Oh, no, o' course not," said Captain Stubbs.

"What do you mean by 'o' course not'?" demanded the indignant master of the John Henry.

"Your deal," said Captain Stubbs, pushing the cards over to him.

"You haven't answered my question," said Captain Thomsett, regarding him offensively.

"There's some questions," said Stubbs slowly, "as is best left unanswered. When you've seen as much law as I have, my lad, you'll know that one of the first principles of English law is, that nobody is bound to commit themselves."

"Do you mean to say you think it is me?" bellowed Captain Thomsett.

"I mean to say nothing," said Captain Stubbs, putting his huge hands on the table. "But when a man comes into my cabin and begins to hum an' haw an' hint at things, and then begins to ask my advice about bigamy, I can't help thinking. This is a free country, and there's no law ag'in thinking. Make a clean breast of it, cap'n, an' I'll do what I can for you."

"You're a blanked fool," said Captain Thomsett wrathfully.

Captain Stubbs shook his head gently, and smiled with infinite patience. "P'raps so," he said modestly. "P'raps so; but there's one thing I can do, and that is, I can read people."

"You can read me, I s'pose?" said Thomsett sneeringly.

"Easy, my lad," said the other, still preserving, though by an obvious effort, his appearance of judicial calm. "I've seen your sort before. One in pertikler I call to mind. He's doing fourteen years now, pore chap. But you needn't be alarmed, cap'n. Your secret is safe enough with me."

Captain Thomsett got up and pranced up and down the cabin, but Captain Stubbs remained calm. He had seen that sort before. It was interesting to the student of human nature, and he regarded his visitor with an air of compassionate interest. Then Captain Thomsett resumed his seat, and, to preserve his own fair fame, betrayed that of George.

"I knew it was either you or somebody your kind 'art was interested in," said the discomfited Stubbs, as they resumed the interrupted game. "You can't help your face, cap'n. When you was thinking about that pore chap's danger it was working with emotion. It misled me, I own it, but it ain't often I meet such a feeling 'art as yours."

Captain Thomsett, his eyes glowing affectionately, gripped his friend's hand, and in the course of the game listened to an exposition of the law relating to bigamy of a most masterly and complicated nature, seasoned with anecdotes calculated to make the hardiest of men pause on the brink of matrimony and think seriously of their position.

"Suppose this woman comes aboard after pore George," said Thomsett. "What's the best thing to be done?"

"The first thing," said Captain Stubbs, "is to gain time. Put her off."

"Off the ship, d'ye mean?" inquired the other.

"No, no," said the jurist "Pretend he's ill and can't see anybody. By gum, I've got it."

He slapped the table with his open hand, and regarded the other triumphantly.

"Let him turn into his bunk and pretend to be dead," he continued, in a voice trembling with pride at his strategy. "It's pretty dark down your foc'sle, I know. Don't have no light down there, and tell him to keep quiet."

Captain Thomsett's eyes shone, but with a qualified admiration.

"Ain't it somewhat sudden?" he demurred.

Captain Stubbs regarded him with a look of supreme artfulness, and slowly closed one eye.

"He got a chill going in the water," he said quietly.

"Well, you're a masterpiece," said Thomsett ungrudgingly. "I will say this of you, you're a masterpiece. Mind this is all to be kept quite secret."

"Make your mind easy," said the eminent jurist. "If I told all I know there's a good many men in this river as 'ud be doing time at the present moment."

Captain Thomsett expressed his pleasure at this information, and, having tried in vain to obtain a few of their names, even going so far as to suggest some, looked at the clock, and, shaking hands, departed to his own ship. Captain Stubbs, left to himself, finished his pipe and retired to rest; and his mate, who had been lying in the adjoining bunk during the consultation, vainly trying to get to sleep, scratched his head, and tried to think of a little strategy himself. He had glimmerings of it before he fell asleep, but when he awoke next morning it flashed before him in all the fulness of its matured beauty.

He went on deck smiling, and, leaning his arms on the side, gazed contemplatively at George, who was sitting on the deck listening darkly to the cook as that worthy read aloud from a newspaper.

"Anything interesting, cook?" demanded the mate.

"About George, sir," said the cook, stopping in his reading. "There's pictures of 'im too."

He crossed to the side, and, handing the paper to the mate, listened smilingly to the little ejaculations of surprise and delight of that deceitful man as he gazed upon the likenesses. "Wonderful," he said emphatically. "Wonderful. I never saw such a good likeness in my life, George. That'll be copied in every newspaper in London, and here's the name in full too—'George Cooper, schooner John Henry, now lying off Limehouse.'"

He handed the paper back to the cook and turned away grinning as George, unable to control himself any longer, got up with an oath and went below to nurse his wrath in silence. A little later the mate of the brig, after a very confidential chat with his own crew, lit his pipe and, with a jaunty air, went ashore.

For the next hour or two George alternated between the foc'sle and the deck, from whence he cast harassed glances at the busy wharves ashore. The skipper, giving it as his own suggestion, acquainted him with the arrangements made in case of the worst, and George, though he seemed somewhat dubious about them, went below and put his bed in order.

"It's very unlikely she'll see that particular newspaper though," said the skipper encouragingly.

"People are sure to see what you don't want 'em to," growled George. "Somebody what knows us is sure to see it, an' show 'er."

"There's a lady stepping into a waterman's skiff now," said the skipper, glancing at the stairs. "That wouldn't be her, I s'pose?"

He turned to the seaman as he spoke, but the words had hardly left his lips before George was going below and undressing for his part.

"If anybody asks for me," he said, turning to the cook, who was regarding his feverish movements in much astonishment, "I'm dead."

"You're wot?" inquired the other.

"Dead," said George. "Dead. Died at ten o'clock this morning. D'ye understand, fat-head?"

"I can't say as 'ow I do," said the cook somewhat acrimoniously.

"Pass the word round that I'm dead," repeated George hurriedly. "Lay me out, cookie. I'll do as much for you one day."

Instead of complying the horrified cook rushed up on deck to tell the skipper that George's brain had gone; but, finding him in the midst of a hurried explanation to the men, stopped with greedy ears to listen. The skiff was making straight for the schooner, propelled by an elderly waterman in his shirt-sleeves, the sole passenger being a lady of ample proportions, who was watching the life of the river through a black veil.

In another minute the skiff bumped alongside, and the waterman standing in the boat passed the painter aboard. The skipper gazed at the fare and, shivering inwardly, hoped that George was a good actor.

"I want to see Mr. Cooper," said the lady grimly, as she clambered aboard, assisted by the waterman.

"I'm very sorry, but you can't see him, mum," said the skipper politely.

"Ho! carn't I?" said the lady, raising her voice a little. "You go an' tell him that his lawful wedded wife, what he deserted, is aboard."

"It 'ud be no good, mum," said the skipper, who felt the full dramatic force of the situation. "I'm afraid he wouldn't listen to you."

"Ho! I think I can persuade 'im a bit," said the lady, drawing in her lips. "Where is 'e?"

"Up aloft," said the skipper, removing his hat.

"Don't you give me none of your lies," said the lady, as she scanned both masts closely.

"He's dead," said the skipper solemnly.

His visitor threw up her arms and staggered back. The cook was nearest, and, throwing his arms round her waist, he caught her as she swayed. The mate, who was of a sympathetic nature, rushed below for whisky, as she sank back on the hatchway, taking the reluctant cook with her.

"Poor thing," said the skipper.

"Don't 'old 'er so tight, cook," said one of the men. "There's no necessity to squeeze 'er."

"Pat 'er 'ands," said another.

"Pat 'em yourself," said the cook brusquely, as he looked up and saw the delight of the crew of the Endeavour, who were leaning over their vessel's side regarding the proceedings with much interest.

"Don't leave go of me," said the newly-made widow, as she swallowed the whisky, and rose to her feet.

"Stand by her, cook," said the skipper authoritatively.

"Ay, ay, sir," said the cook.

They formed a procession below, the skipper and mate leading; the cook with his fair burden, choking her sobs with a handkerchief, and the crew following.

"What did he die of?" she asked in a whisper broken with sobs.

"Chill from the water," whispered the skipper in response.

"I can't see 'im," she whispered. "It's so dark here. Has anybody got a match? Oh! here's some."

Before anybody could interfere she took a box from a locker, and, striking one, bent over the motionless George, and gazed at his tightly-closed eyes and open mouth in silence.

"You'll set the bed alight," said the mate in a low voice, as the end of the match dropped off.

"It won't hurt 'im," whispered the widow tearfully.

The mate, who had distinctly seen the corpse shift a bit, thought differently.

"Nothing 'll 'urt 'im now" whispered the widow, sniffing as she struck another match. "Oh! if he could only sit up 'and speak to me."

For a moment the mate, who knew George's temper, thought it highly probable that he would, as the top of the second match fell between his shirt and his neck.

"Don't look any more," said the skipper anxiously; "you can't do him any good."

His visitor handed him the matches, and, for a short time, sobbed in silence.

"We've done all we could for him," said the skipper at length. "It 'ud be best for you to go home and lay down a bit."

"You're all very good, I'm sure," whispered the widow, turning away. "I'll send for him this evening."

They all started, especially the corpse.

"Eh?" said the skipper.

"He was a bad 'usband to me," she continued, still in the same sobbing whisper, "but I'll 'ave 'im put away decent."

"You'd better let us bury him," said the skipper. "We can do it cheaper than you can, perhaps?"

"No. I'll send for him this evening," said the lady. "Are they 'is clothes?"

"The last he ever wore," said the skipper pathetically, pointing to the heap of clothing. "There's his chest, pore chap, just as he left it."

The bereaved widow bent down, and, raising the lid, shook her head tearfully as she regarded the contents. Then she gathered up the clothes under her left arm, and, still sobbing, took his watch, his knife, and some small change from his chest, while the crew in dumb show inquired of the deceased, who was regarding her over the edge of the bunk, what was to be done.

"I suppose there was some money due to him?" she inquired, turning to the skipper.

"Matter of a few shillings," he stammered.

"I'll take them," she said, holding out her hand.

The skipper put his hand in his pocket and, in his turn, looked inquiringly at the late lamented for guidance; but George had closed his eyes again to the world, and, after a moment's hesitation, he slowly counted the money into her hand.

She dropped the coins into her pocket, and, with a parting glance at the motionless figure in the bunk, turned away. The procession made its way on deck again, but not in the same order, the cook carefully bringing up the rear.

"If there's any other little things," she said, pausing at the side to get a firmer grip of the clothes under her arm.

"You shall have them," said the skipper, who had been making mental arrangements to have George buried before her return.

Apparently much comforted by this assurance, she allowed herself to be lowered into the boat, which was waiting. The excitement of the crew of the brig, who had been watching her movements with eager interest, got beyond the bounds of all decency as they saw her being pulled ashore with the clothes in her lap.

"You can come up now," said the skipper, as he caught sight of George's face at the scuttle.

"Has she gone?" inquired the seaman anxiously.

The skipper nodded, and a wild cheer rose from the crew of the brig as George came on deck in his scanty garments, and from behind the others peered cautiously over the side.

"Where is she?" he demanded.

The skipper pointed to the boat.

"That?" said George, starting. "That? That ain't my wife."

"Not your wife?" said the skipper, staring. "Whose is she then?"

"How the devil should I know?" said George, throwing discipline to the winds in his agitation. "It ain't my wife."

"P'raps it's one you've forgotten," suggested the skipper in a low voice.

George looked at him and choked. "I've never seen her before," he replied, "s'elp me. Call her back. Stop her."

The mate rushed aft and began to haul in the ship's boat, but George caught him suddenly by the arm.

"Never mind," he said bitterly; "better let her go. She seems to know too much for me. Somebody's been talking to her."

It was the same thought that was troubling the skipper, and he looked searchingly from one to the other for an explanation. He fancied that he saw it when he met the eye of the mate of the brig, and he paused irresolutely as the skiff reached the stairs, and the woman, springing ashore, waved the clothes triumphantly in the direction of the schooner and disappeared.

THE UNDERSTUDY

"Dogs on board ship is a nuisance," said the night-watchman, gazing fiercely at the vociferous mongrel that had chased him from the deck of the Henry William; "the skipper asks me to keep an eye on the ship, and then leaves a thing like that down in the cabin."

He leaned against a pile of empty casks to recover his breath, shook his fist at the dog, and said, slowly—

Some people can't make too much of 'em. They talk about a dog's honest eyes and his faithful 'art. I 'ad a dog once, and I never saw his eyes look so honest as they did one day when 'e was sitting on a pound o' beefsteak we was 'unting high and low for.

I've known dogs to cause a lot of trouble in my time. A man as used to live in my street told me he 'ad been in jail three times because dogs follered him 'ome and wouldn't go away when he told 'em to. He said that some men would ha' kicked 'em out into the street, but he thought their little lives was far too valuable to risk in that way.

Some people used to wink when 'e talked like that, but I didn't: I remembered a dog that took a fancy to old Sam Small and Ginger Dick and Peter Russet once in just the same way.

It was one night in a little public-'ouse down Commercial Road way. They 'ad on'y been ashore a week, and, 'aving been turned out of a music-'all the night afore because a man Ginger Dick had punched in the jaw wouldn't behave 'imself, they said they'd spend the rest o' their money on beer instead. There was just the three of 'em sitting by themselves in a cosy little bar, when the door was pushed open and a big black dog came in.

He came straight up to Sam and licked his 'and. Sam was eating a arrowroot biscuit with a bit o' cheese on it at the time. He wasn't wot you'd call a partickler sort o' man, but, seeing as 'ow the dog was so careless that 'e licked the biscuit a'most as much as he did his 'and, he gave it to 'im. The dog took it in one gulp, and then he jumped up on Sam's lap and wagged his tail in 'is face for joy and thankfulness.

"He's took a fancy to you, Sam," ses Ginger.

Sam pushed the dog off on to the floor and wiped his face.

"He's a good dog, by the look of 'im," ses Peter Russet, who was country bred.

He bought a sausage-roll, and him and the dog ate it between 'em. Then Ginger Dick bought one and gave it to 'im, and by the time it was finished the dog didn't seem to know which one of 'em he loved the most.

"Wonder who he belongs to?" ses Ginger. "Is there any name on the collar, Peter?"

Peter shook his 'ead. "It's a good collar, though," he ses. "I wonder whether he's been and lost 'imself?"

Old Sam, wot was always on the look-out for money, put his beer down and wiped 'is mouth. "There might be a reward out for 'im," he ses. "I think I'll take care of 'im for a day or two, in case."

"We'll all take care of 'im," ses Ginger; "and if there's a reward we'll go shares. Mind that!"

"I found 'im," ses Sam, very disagreeable. "He came up to me as if he'd known me all 'is life."

"No," ses Ginger. "Don't you flatter yourself. He came up to you because he didn't know you, Sam."

"If he 'ad, he'd ha' bit your 'and," ses Peter Russet.

"Instead o' washing it," ses Ginger.

"Go on!" ses Sam, 'olding his breath with passion. "Go on!"

Peter opened 'is mouth, but just then another man came into the bar, and, arter ordering 'is drink, turned round and patted the dog's 'ead.

"That's a good dog; 'ow old is he?" he ses to Ginger.

"Two years last April," ses Ginger, without moving a eyelid.

"Fifth of April," ses old Sam, very quick and fierce.

"At two o'clock in the morning," ses Peter.

The man took up 'is beer and looked at 'em; then 'e took a drink and looked at 'em again. Arter which he 'ad another look at the dog.

"I could see 'e was very valuable," he ses. "I see that the moment I set eyes on 'im. Mind you don't get 'im stole."

He finished up 'is beer and went out; and he 'ad 'ardly gone afore Ginger took a piece o' thick string out of 'is pocket and fastened it to the dog's collar.

"Make yourself at 'ome, Ginger," ses Sam, very nasty.

"I'm going to," ses Ginger. "That chap knows something about dogs, and, if we can't get a reward for 'im, p'r'aps we can sell 'im."

They 'ad another arf-pint each, and then, Ginger taking 'old of the string, they went out into the street.

"Nine o'clock," ses Peter. "It's no good going 'ome yet, Ginger."

"We can 'ave a glass or two on the way," ses Ginger; "but I sha'n't feel comfortable in my mind till we've got the dog safe 'ome. P'r'aps the people wot 'ave lost it are looking for it now."

They 'ad another drink farther on, and a man in the bar took such a fancy to the dog that 'e offered Ginger five shillings for it and drinks round.

"That shows 'ow valuable it is," ses Peter Russet when they got outside. "Hold that string tight, Ginger. Wot's the matter?"

"He won't come," ses Ginger, tugging at the string. "Come on, old chap! Good dog! Come on!"

He stood there pulling at the dog, wot was sitting down and being dragged along on its stummick. He didn't know its name, but 'e called it a few things that seemed to ease 'is mind, and then he 'anded over the string to Sam, wot 'ad been asking for it, and told 'im to see wot he could do.

"We shall 'ave a crowd round us in a minute," ses Peter. "Mind you don't bust a blood-vessel, Sam."

"And be locked up for stealing it, p'r'aps," ses Ginger. "Better let it go, Sam."

"Wot, arter refusing five bob for it?" ses Sam. "Talk sense, Ginger, and give it a shove be'ind."

Ginger gave it a shove, but it was no good. There was three or four people coming along the road, and Sam made up 'is mind in an instant, and 'eld up his 'and to a cab that was passing.

It took the three of 'em to get the dog into the cab, and as soon as it was in the cabman told 'em to take it out agin. They argufied with 'im till their tongues ached, and at last, arter paying 'im four shillings and sixpence afore they started, he climbed up on the box and drove off.

The door was open when they got to their lodgings, but they 'ad to be careful because o' the landlady. It took the three of 'em to pull and push that dog upstairs, and Ginger took a dislike to dogs that 'e never really got over. They got 'im in the bedroom at last, and, arter they 'ad given 'im a drink o' water out o' the wash-hand basin, Ginger and Peter started to find fault with Sam Small.

"I know wot I'm about," ses Sam; "but, o' course, if you don't want your share, say so. Wot?"

"Talk sense!" ses Ginger. "We paid our share o' the cab, didn't we? And more fools us."

"There won't be no share," ses Peter Russet; "but if there is, we're going to 'ave it."

They undressed themselves and got into bed, and Ginger 'adn't been in his five minutes afore the dog started to get in with 'im. When Ginger pushed 'im off 'e seemed to think he was having a game with 'im, and, arter pretending to bite 'im in play, he took the end of the counterpane in 'is mouth and tried to drag it off.

"Why don't you get to sleep, Ginger?" ses Sam, who was just dropping off. "'Ave a game with 'im in the morning."

Ginger gave the dog a punch in the chest, and, arter saying a few o' the things he'd like to do to Sam Small, he cuddled down in 'is bed and they all went off to sleep. All but the dog, that is. He seemed uneasy in 'is mind, and if 'e woke 'em up once by standing on his 'ind-legs and putting his fore-paws on their chest to see if they was still alive, he did arf-a-dozen times.

He dropped off to sleep at last, scratching 'imself, but about three o'clock in the morning Ginger woke up with a 'orrible start and sat up in bed shivering. Sam and Peter woke up, too, and, raising themselves in bed, looked at the dog, wot was sitting on its tail, with its 'ead back, moaning fit to break its 'art.

"Wot's the matter?" ses old Sam, in a shaky voice. "Stop it! Stop it, d'ye hear!"

"P'r'aps it's dying," ses Ginger, as the dog let off a 'owl like a steamer coming up the river. "Stop it, you brute!"

"He'll wake the 'ouse up in a minute," ses Peter. "Take 'im downstairs and kick 'im into the street, Sam."

"Take 'im yourself," ses Sam. "Hsh! Somebody's coming upstairs. Poor old doggie. Come along, then. Come along."

The dog left off his 'owling, and went over and licked 'im just as the landlady and one or two more came to the door and called out to know wot they meant by it.

"It's all right, missis," ses Sam. "It's on'y pore Ginger. You keep quiet," he ses in a whisper, turning to Ginger.

"Wot's he making that row about?" ses the landlady. "He made my blood run cold."

"He's got a touch o' toothache," ses Sam. "Never mind, Ginger," 'e ses in a hurry, as the dog let off another 'owl; "try and bear it."

"He's a coward, that's wot 'e is," ses the landlady, very fierce. "Why, a child o' five wouldn't make such a fuss."

"Sounds more like a dog than a 'uman being," ses another voice. "You come outside, Ginger, and I'll give you something to cry for."

They waited a minute or two, and then, everything being quiet, they went back to bed, while old Sam talked to Ginger about wot 'e called 'is "presence o' mind," and Ginger talked to 'im about wot he'd do to 'im if 'e wasn't a fat old man with one foot in the grave.

They was all in a better temper when they woke up in the morning, and while Sam was washing they talked about wot they was to do with the dog.

"We can't lead 'im about all day," ses Ginger; "and if we let 'im off the string he'll go off 'ome."

"He don't know where his 'ome is," ses Sam, very severe; "but he might run away, and then the pore thing might be starved or else ill-treated. I 'ave 'eard o' boys tying tin cans to their tails."

"I've done it myself," ses Ginger, nodding. "Consequently it's our dooty to look arter 'im," ses Sam.

"I'll go down to the front door," ses Peter, "and when I whistle, bring him down."

Ginger stuck his 'ead out o' the window, and by and by, when Peter whistled, him and Sam took the dog downstairs and out into the street.

"So far so good," ses Sam; "now, wot about brekfuss?"

They 'ad their brekfuss in their usual coffeeshop, and the dog took bits from all of them. Unfortunately, 'e wasn't used to haddick bones, and arter two of the customers 'ad gorn out and two more 'ad complained to the landlord, they 'ad to leave their brekfusses and take 'im outside for a breath o' fresh air.

"Now, wot are we going to do?" ses Ginger. "I'm beginning to be sick of the sight of 'im. 'Ave we got to lead 'im about all day on a bit o' string?"

"Let's take 'im round the corner and lose 'im," ses Peter Russet.

"You give me 'old o' that string," ses Sam. "If you don't want shares, that's all right. If I'm going to look arter 'im I'll 'ave it all."

That made Ginger and Peter look at each other. Direckly Sam began to talk about money they began to think they might be losing something.

"And wot about 'aving 'im in our bedroom and keeping us awake all night?" ses Peter.

"And putting it on to me with the toothache," ses Ginger. "No; you can look arter 'im, Sam, while me and Peter goes off and enjoys ourselves; and if you get anything we go shares, mind."

"All right," ses Sam, turning away with the dog.

"And suppose Sam gets a reward or sells it, and then tells us that it ran away and 'e lost it?" ses Peter.

"O' course; I never thought o' that," ses Ginger. "You've got your 'ead on straight, Peter."

"I see 'im smile, that's why," ses Peter Russet.

"You're a liar," ses Sam.

"We'll stick together," ses Ginger. "Leastways, one of us'll keep with you, Sam."

They settled it that way at last, and while Ginger went for a walk down round about where they 'ad found the dog, Sam Small and Peter waited for him in a little public-'ouse down Limehouse way. Their idea was that there would be bills up, and when Ginger came back and said there wasn't, they 'ad a lot to say about people wot wasn't fit to 'ave dogs because they didn't love 'em.

They 'ad a miserable day. When the dog got sick o' sitting in a pub 'e made such a noise they 'ad to take 'im out; and when 'e got tired o' walking about he sat down on the pavement and they 'ad to drag 'im along to the nearest pub agin. At five o'clock in the arternoon Ginger Dick was talking about two-penn'orth o' rat-poison.

"Wot are we to do with 'im till twelve o'clock to-night?" ses Peter.

"And s'pose we can't smuggle 'im into the 'ouse agin?" ses Ginger. "Or suppose he makes that noise agin in the night?"

They 'ad a pint each to 'elp them to think wot was to be done. And, arter a lot o' talking and quarrelling, they did wot a lot of other people 'ave done when they got into trouble: they came to me.

I 'ad on'y been on dooty about arf an hour when the three of 'em turned up at the wharf with the dog, and, arter saying 'ow well I looked and that I seemed to get younger every time they saw me, they asked me to take charge of the dog for 'em.

"It'll be company for you," ses old Sam. "It must be very lonely 'ere of a night. I've often thought of it."

"And of a day-time you could take it 'ome and tie it up in your back-yard," ses Ginger.

I wouldn't 'ave anything to do with it at fust, but at last I gave way. They offered me fourpence a day for its keep, and, as I didn't want to run any risk, I made 'em give me a couple o' bob to go on with.

They went off as though they'd left a load o' care be'ind 'em, and arter tying the dog up to a crane I went on with my work. They 'adn't told me wot the game was, but, from one or two things they'd let drop, I'd got a pretty good idea.

The dog 'owled a bit at fust, but he quieted down arter a bit. He was a nice-looking animal, but one dog is much the same as another to me, and if I 'ad one ten years I don't suppose I could pick it out from two or three others.

I took it off 'ome with me when I left at six o'clock next morning, and tied it up in my yard. My missis 'ad words about it, o' course—that's wot people get married for—but when she found it woke me up three times she quieted down and said wot a nice coat it 'ad got.

The three of 'em came round next evening to see it, and they was so afraid of its being lost that when they stood me a pint at the Bull's Head we 'ad to take it with us. Ginger was going to buy a sausage-roll for it, but, arter Sam 'ad pointed out that they was paying me fourpence a day for its keep, he didn't. And Sam 'ad the cheek to tell me that it liked a nice bit o' fried steak as well as anything.

A lot o' people admired that dog. I remember, on the fourth night I think it was, the barge Dauntless came alongside, and arter she was made fast the skipper came ashore and took a little notice of it.

"Where did you get 'im?" he ses.

I told 'im 'ow it was, and he stood there for some time patting the dog on the 'ead and whistling under 'is breath.

"It's much the same size as my dog," he ses; "that's a black retriever, too."

I ses "Oh!"

"I'm afraid I shall 'ave to get rid of it," he ses. "It's on the barge now. My missis won't 'ave it in the 'ouse any more cos it bit the baby. And o' course it was no good p'inting out to 'er that it was its first bite. Even the law allows one bite, but it's no good talking about the law to wimmen."

"Except when it's on their side," I ses.

He patted the dog's 'ead agin and whistled, and a big black dog came up out of the cabin and sprang ashore. It went up and put its nose to Sam's dog, and they both growled like thunderstorms.

"Might be brothers," ses the skipper, "on'y your dog's got a better 'eead and a better coat. It's a good dog."

"They're all alike to me," I ses. "I couldn't tell 'em apart, not if you paid me."

The skipper stood there a moment, and then he ses: "I wish you'd let me see 'ow my dog looks in your dog's collar," he ses.

"Whaffor?" I ses.

"On'y fancy," he ses. "Oh, Bill!"

"Yes," I ses.

"It ain't Christmas," he ses, taking my arm and walking up and down a bit, "but it will be soon, and then I mightn't see you. You've done me one or two good turns, and I should like to make you a Christmas-box of three 'arf-dollars."

I let 'im give 'em to me, and then, just to please 'im, I let 'im try the collar on 'is dog, while I swept up a bit.

"It looked beautiful on 'im," he ses, when I'd finished; "but I've put it back agin. Come on, Bruno. Good-night, Bill."

He got 'is dog on the barge agin arter a bit o' trouble, and arter making sure 'that my dog 'ad got its own collar on I went on with my work.

The dog didn't seem to be quite 'imself next day, and he was so fierce in the yard that my missis was afraid to go near 'im. I was going to ask the skipper about it, as 'e seemed to know more about dogs than I did, but when I got to the wharf the barge had sailed.

It was just getting dark when there came a ring at the gate-bell, and afore I could answer it arf-a-dozen more, as fast as the bell could go. And when I opened the wicket Sam Small and Ginger and Peter Russet all tried to get in at once.

"Where's the dog?" ses Sam.

"Tied up," I ses. "Wot's the matter? 'Ave you all gorn mad?"

They didn't answer me. They ran on to the jetty, and afore I could turn round a'most they 'ad got the dog loose and was dragging it towards me, smiling all over their faces.

"Reward," ses Ginger, as I caught 'old of 'im by the coat. "Five pounds —landlord of a pub—at Bow— come on, Sam!"

"Why don't you keep your mouth shut, Ginger?" ses Sam.

"Five pounds!" I ses. "Five pounds! Hurrah!"

"Wot are you hurraying about?" ses Sam, very short.

"Why," I ses, "I s'pose—Here, arf a moment!"

"Can't stop," ses Sam, going arter the others.

I watched 'em up the road, and then I locked the gate and walked up and down the wharf thinking wot a funny thing money is, and 'ow it alters people's natures. And arter all, I thought that three arf-dollars earned honest was better than a reward for hiding another man's dog.

I finished tidying up, and at nine o'clock I went into the office for a quiet smoke. I couldn't 'elp wondering 'ow them three 'ad got on, and just as I was thinking about it there came the worst ringing at the gate-bell I 'ave ever 'eard in my life, and the noise of heavy boots kicking the gate. It was so violent I 'ardly liked to go at fust, thinking it might be bad news, but I opened it at last, and in bust Sam Small, with Ginger and Peter.

For five minutes they all talked at once, with their nasty fists 'eld under my nose. I couldn't make lead or tail of it at fust, and then I found as 'ow they 'ad got the dog back with them, and that the landlord 'ad said 'e wasn't the one.

"But 'e said as he thought the collar was his," ses Sam. "'Ow do you account for that?"

"P'r'aps he made a mistake," I ses; "or p'r'aps he thought you'd turn the dog adrift and he'd get it back for nothing. You know wot landlords are. Try 'im agin."

"I'd pretty well swear he ain't the same dog," ses Peter Russet, looking in a puzzled way at Sam and Ginger.

"You take 'im back to-morrow night," I ses. "It's a nice walk to Bow. And then come back and beg my pardon. I want to 'ave a word with this policeman here. Goodnight."

THE UNKNOWN

"Handsome is as 'andsome does," said the night-watchman. It's an old saying, but it's true. Give a chap good looks, and it's precious little else that is given to 'im. He's lucky when 'is good looks 'ave gorn—or partly gorn—to get a berth as night-watchman or some other hard and bad-paid job.

One drawback to a good-looking man is that he generally marries young; not because 'e wants to, but because somebody else wants 'im to. And that ain't the worst of it: the handsomest chap I ever knew married five times, and got seven years for it. It wasn't his fault, pore chap; he simply couldn't say No.

One o' the best-looking men I ever knew was Cap'n Bill Smithers, wot used to come up here once a week with a schooner called the Wild Rose. Funny thing about 'im was he didn't seem to know about 'is good looks, and he was one o' the quietest, best-behaved men that ever came up the London river. Considering that he was mistook for me more than once, it was just as well.

He didn't marry until 'e was close on forty; and then 'e made the mistake of marrying a widder-woman. She was like all the rest of 'em—only worse. Afore she was married butter wouldn't melt in 'er mouth, but as soon as she 'ad got her "lines" safe she began to make up for it.

For the fust month or two 'e didn't mind it, 'e rather liked being fussed arter, but when he found that he couldn't go out for arf an hour without having 'er with 'im he began to get tired of it. Her idea was that 'e was too handsome to be trusted out alone; and every trip he made 'e had to write up in a book, day by day, wot 'e did with himself. Even then she wasn't satisfied, and, arter saying that a wife's place was by the side of 'er husband, she took to sailing with 'im every v'y'ge.

Wot he could ha' seen in 'er I don't know. I asked 'im one evening—in a roundabout way—and he answered in such a long, roundabout way that I didn't know wot to make of it till I see that she was standing just behind me, listening. Arter that I heard 'er asking questions about me, but I didn't 'ave to listen: I could hear 'er twenty yards away, and singing to myself at the same time.

Arter that she treated me as if I was the dirt beneath 'er feet. She never spoke to me, but used to speak against me to other people. She was always talking to them about the "sleeping-sickness" and things o' that kind. She said night-watchmen always made 'er think of it somehow, but she didn't know why, and she couldn't tell you if you was to ask her. The only thing I was thankful for was that I wasn't 'er husband. She stuck to 'im like his shadow, and I began to think at last it was a pity she 'adn't got some thing to be jealous about and something to occupy her mind with instead o' me.

"She ought to 'ave a lesson," I ses to the skipper one evening. "Are you going to be follered about like this all your life? If she was made to see the foolishness of 'er ways she might get sick of it."

My idea was to send her on a wild-goose chase, and while the Wild Rose was away I thought it out. I wrote a love-letter to the skipper signed with the name of "Dorothy," and asked 'im to meet me at Cleopatra's Needle on the Embankment at eight o'clock on Wednesday. I told 'im to look out for a tall girl (Mrs. Smithers was as short as they make 'em) with mischievous brown eyes, in a blue 'at with red roses on it.

I read it over careful, and arter marking it "Private," twice in front and once on the back, I stuck it down so that it could be blown open a'most, and waited for the schooner to come back. Then I gave a van-boy twopence to 'and it to Mrs. Smithers, wot was sitting on the deck alone, and tell 'er it was a letter for Captain Smithers.

I was busy with a barge wot happened to be handy at the time, but I 'eard her say that she would take it and give it to 'im. When I peeped round she 'ad got the letter open and was leaning over the side to wind'ard trying to get 'er breath. Every now and then she'd give another look at the letter and open 'er mouth and gasp; but by and by she got calmer, and, arter putting it back in the envelope, she gave it a lick as though she was going to bite it, and stuck it down agin. Then she went off the wharf, and I'm blest if, five minutes arterwards, a young fellow didn't come down to the ship with the same letter and ask for the skipper.

"Who gave it you?" ses the skipper, as soon as 'e could speak.

"A lady," ses the young fellow.

The skipper waved 'im away, and then 'e walked up and down the deck like a man in a dream.

"Bad news?" I ses, looking up and catching 'is eye.

"No," he ses, "no. Only a note about a couple o' casks o' soda."

He stuffed the letter in 'is pocket and sat on the side smoking till his wife came back in five minutes' time, smiling all over with good temper.

"It's a nice evening," she ses, "and I think I'll just run over to Dalston and see my Cousin Joe."

The skipper got up like a lamb and said he'd go and clean 'imself.

"You needn't come if you feel tired," she ses, smiling at 'im.

The skipper could 'ardly believe his ears.

"I do feel tired," he ses. "I've had a heavy day, and I feel more like bed than anything else."

"You turn in, then," she ses. "I'll be all right by myself."

She went down and tidied herself up—not that it made much difference to 'er—and, arter patting him on the arm and giving me a stare that would ha' made most men blink, she took herself off.

I was pretty busy that evening. Wot with shifting lighters from under the jetty and sweeping up, it was pretty near ha'-past seven afore I 'ad a minute I could call my own. I put down the broom at last, and was just thinking of stepping round to the Bull's Head for a 'arf-pint when I see Cap'n Smithers come off the ship on to the wharf and walk to the gate.

"I thought you was going to turn in?" I ses.

"I did think of it," he ses, "then I thought p'r'aps I'd better stroll as far as Broad Street and meet my wife."

It was all I could do to keep a straight face. I'd a pretty good idea where she 'ad gorn; and it wasn't Dalston.

"Come in and 'ave 'arf a pint fust," I ses.

"No; I shall be late," he ses, hurrying off.

I went in and 'ad a glass by myself, and stood there so long thinking of Mrs. Smithers walking up and down by Cleopatra's Needle that at last the landlord fust asked me wot I was laughing at, and then offered to make me laugh the other side of my face. And then he wonders why people go to the Albion.

I locked the gate rather earlier than usual that night. Sometimes if I'm up that end I leave it a bit late, but I didn't want Mrs. Smithers to come along and nip in without me seeing her face.

It was ten o'clock afore I heard the bell go, and when I opened the wicket and looked out I was surprised to see that she 'ad got the skipper with 'er. And of all the miserable-looking objects I ever saw in my life he was the worst. She 'ad him tight by the arm, and there was a look on 'er face that a'most scared me.

"Did you go all the way to Dalston for her?" I ses to 'im.

Mrs. Smithers made a gasping sort o' noise, but the skipper didn't answer a word.

She shoved him in in front of 'er and stood ever 'im while he climbed aboard. When he held out 'is hand to help 'er she struck it away.

I didn't get word with 'im till five o'clock next morning, when he came up on deck with his 'air all rough and 'is eyes red for want of sleep.

"Haven't 'ad a wink all night," he ses, stepping on to the wharf.

I gave a little cough. "Didn't she 'ave a pleasant time at Dalston?" I ses.

He walked a little further off from the ship. "She didn't go there," he ses, in a whisper.

"You've got something on your mind," I ses. "Wot is it?"

He wouldn't tell me at fust, but at last he told me all about the letter from Dorothy, and 'is wife reading it unbeknown to 'im and going to meet 'er.

"It was an awful meeting!" he ses. "Awful!"

I couldn't think wot to make of it. "Was the gal there, then?" I ses, staring at 'im.

"No," ses the skipper; "but I was."

"You?" I ses, starting back. "You! Wot for? I'm surprised at you! I wouldn't ha' believed it of you!"

"I felt a bit curious," he ses, with a silly sort o' smile. "But wot I can't understand is why the gal didn't turn up."

"I'm ashamed of you, Bill," I ses, very severe.

"P'r'aps she did," he ses, 'arf to 'imself, "and then saw my missis standing there waiting. P'r'aps that was it."

"Or p'r'aps it was somebody 'aving a game with you," I ses.

"You're getting old, Bill," he ses, very short. "You don't understand. It's some pore gal that's took a fancy to me, and it's my dooty to meet 'er and tell her 'ow things are."

He walked off with his 'ead in the air, and if 'e took that letter out once and looked at it, he did five times.

"Chuck it away," I ses, going up to him.

"Certainly not," he ses, folding it up careful and stowing it away in 'is breastpocket. "She's took a fancy to me, and it's my dooty—"

"You said that afore," I ses.

He stared at me nasty for a moment, and then 'e ses: "You ain't seen any young lady hanging about 'ere, I suppose, Bill? A tall young lady with a blue hat trimmed with red roses?"

I shook my 'ead.

"If you should see 'er" he ses.

"I'll tell your missis," I ses. "It 'ud be much easier for her to do her dooty properly than it would you. She'd enjoy doing it, too."

He went off agin then, and I thought he 'ad done with me, but he 'adn't. He spoke to me that evening as if I was the greatest friend he 'ad in the world. I 'ad two 'arfpints with 'im at the Albion— with his missis walking up and down outside—and arter the second 'arf-pint he said he wanted to meet Dorothy and tell 'er that 'e was married, and that he 'oped she would meet some good man that was worthy of 'er.

I had a week's peace while the ship was away, but she was hardly made fast afore I 'ad it all over agin and agin.

"Are you sure there's been no more letters?" he ses.

"Sartain," I ses.

"That's right," he ses; "that's right. And you 'aven't seen her walking up and down?"

"No," I ses.

"'Ave you been on the look-out?" he ses. "I don't suppose a nice gal like that would come and shove her 'ead in at the gate. Did you look up and down the road?"

"Yes," I ses. "I've fair made my eyes ache watching for her."

"I can't understand it," he ses. "It's a mystery to me, unless p'r'aps she's been taken ill. She must 'ave seen me here in the fust place; and she managed to get hold of my name. Mark my words, I shall 'ear from her agin."

"'Ow do you know?" I ses.

"I feel it 'ere," he ses, very solemn, laying his 'and on his chest.

I didn't know wot to do. Wot with 'is foolishness and his missis's temper, I see I 'ad made a mess of it. He told me she had 'ardly spoke a word to 'im for two days, and when I said—being a married man myself— that it might ha' been worse, 'e said I didn't know wot I was talking about.

I did a bit o' thinking arter he 'ad gorn aboard agin. I dursn't tell 'im that I 'ad wrote the letter, but I thought if he 'ad one or two more he'd see that some one was 'aving a game with 'im, and that it might do 'im good. Besides which it was a little amusement for me.

Arter everybody was in their beds asleep I sat on a clerk's stool in the office and wrote 'im another letter from Dorothy. I called 'im "Dear Bill," and I said 'ow sorry I was that I 'adn't had even a sight of 'im lately, having been laid up with a sprained ankle and 'ad only just got about agin. I asked 'im to meet me at Cleopatra's Needle at eight o'clock, and said that I should wear the blue 'at with red roses.

It was a very good letter, but I can see now that I done wrong in writing it. I was going to post it to 'im, but, as I couldn't find an envelope without the name of the blessed wharf on it, I put it in my pocket till I got 'ome.

I got 'ome at about a quarter to seven, and slept like a child till pretty near four. Then I went downstairs to 'ave my dinner.

The moment I opened the door I see there was something wrong. Three times my missis licked 'er lips afore she could speak. Her face 'ad gone a dirty white colour, and she was leaning forward with her 'ands on her 'ips, trembling all over with temper.

"Is my dinner ready?" I ses, easy-like. "'Cos I'm ready for it."

"I—I wonder I don't tear you limb from limb," she ses, catching her breath.

"Wot's the matter?" I ses.

"And then boil you," she ses, between her teeth. "You in one pot and your precious Dorothy in another."

If anybody 'ad offered me five pounds to speak then, I couldn't ha' done it. I see wot I'd done in a flash, and I couldn't say a word; but I kept my presence o' mind, and as she came round one side o' the table I went round the other.

"Wot 'ave you got to say for yourself?" she ses, with a scream.

"Nothing," I ses, at last. "It's all a mistake."

"Mistake?" she ses. "Yes, you made a mistake leaving it in your pocket; that's all the mistake you've made. That's wot you do, is it, when you're supposed to be at the wharf? Go about with a blue 'at with red roses in it! At your time o' life, and a wife at 'ome working herself to death to make both ends meet and keep you respectable!"

"It's all a mistake," I ses. "The letter wasn't for me."

"Oh, no, o' course not," she ses. "That's why you'd got it in your pocket, I suppose. And I suppose you'll say your name ain't Bill next."

"Don't say things you'll be sorry for," I ses.

"I'll take care o' that," she ses. "I might be sorry for not saying some things, but I don't think I shall."

I don't think she was. I don't think she forgot anything, and she raked up things that I 'ad contradicted years ago and wot I thought was all forgot. And every now and then, when she stopped for breath, she'd try and get round to the same side of the table I was.

She follered me to the street door when I went and called things up the road arter me. I 'ad a snack at a coffee-shop for my dinner, but I 'adn't got much appetite for it; I was too full of trouble and finding fault with myself, and I went off to my work with a 'art as heavy as lead.

I suppose I 'adn't been on the wharf ten minutes afore Cap'n Smithers came sidling up to me, but I got my spoke in fust.

"Look 'ere," I ses, "if you're going to talk about that forward hussy wot's been writing to you, I ain't. I'm sick and tired of 'er."

"Forward hussy!" he ses. "Forward hussy!" And afore I could drop my broom he gave me a punch in the jaw that pretty near broke it. "Say another word against her," he ses, "and I'll knock your ugly 'ead off. How dare you insult a lady?"

I thought I should 'ave gone crazy at fust, but I went off into the office without a word. Some men would ha' knocked 'im down for it, but I made allowances for 'is state o' mind, and I stayed inside until I see 'im get aboard agin.

He was sitting on deck when I went out, and his missis too, but neither of 'em spoke a word. I picked up my broom and went on sweeping, when suddenly I 'eard a voice at the gate I thought I knew, and in came my wife.

"Ho!" she ses, calling out. "Ain't you gone to meet that gal at Cleopatra's Needle yet? You ain't going to keep 'er waiting, are you?"

"H'sh!" I ses.

"H'sh! yourself," she ses, shouting. "I've done nothing to be ashamed of. I don't go to meet other people's husbands in a blue 'at with red roses. I don't write 'em love-letters, and say 'H'sh!' to my wife when she ventures to make a remark about it. I may work myself to skin and bone for a man wot's old enough to know better, but I'm not going to be trod on. Dorothy, indeed! I'll Dorothy 'er if I get the chance."

Mrs. Smithers, wot 'ad been listening with all her ears, jumped up, and so did the skipper, and Mrs. Smithers came to the side in two steps.

"Did you say 'Dorothy,' ma'am?" she ses to my missis.

"I did," ses my wife. "She's been writing to my husband."

"It must be the same one," ses Mrs. Smithers. "She's been writing to mine too."

The two of 'em stood there looking at each other for a minute, and then my wife, holding the letter between 'er finger and thumb as if it was pison, passed it to Mrs. Smithers.

"It's the same," ses Mrs. Smithers. "Was the envelope marked 'Private'?"

"I didn't see no envelope," ses my missis. "This is all I found."

Mrs. Smithers stepped on to the wharf and, taking 'old of my missis by the arm, led her away whispering. At the same moment the skipper walked across the deck and whispered to me.

"Wot d'ye mean by it?" he ses. "Wot d'ye mean by 'aving letters from Dorothy and not telling me about it?"

"I can't help 'aving letters any more than you can," I ses. "Now p'r'aps you'll understand wot I meant by calling 'er a forward hussy."

"Fancy 'er writing to you!" he ses, wrinkling 'is forehead. "Pph! She must be crazy."

"P'r'aps it ain't a gal at all," I ses. "My belief is somebody is 'aving a game with us."

"Don't be a fool," he ses. "I'd like to see the party as would make a fool of me like that. Just see 'im and get my 'ands on him. He wouldn't want to play any more games."

It was no good talking to 'im. He was 'arf crazy with temper. If I'd said the letter was meant for 'im he'd 'ave asked me wot I meant by opening it and getting 'im into more trouble with 'is missis, instead of giving it to 'im on the quiet. I just stood and suffered in silence, and thought wot a lot of 'arm eddication did for people.

"I want some money," ses my missis, coming back at last with Mrs. Smithers.

That was the way she always talked when she'd got me in 'er power. She took two-and-tenpence— all I'd got—and then she ordered me to go and get a cab.

"Me and this lady are going to meet her," she ses, sniffing at me.

"And tell her wot we think of 'er," ses Mrs. Smithers, sniffing too.

"And wot we'll do to 'er," ses my missis.

I left 'em standing side by side, looking at the skipper as if 'e was a waxworks, while I went to find a cab. When I came back they was in the same persition, and 'e was smoking with 'is eyes shut.

They went off side by side in the cab, both of 'em sitting bolt-upright, and only turning their 'eads at the last moment to give us looks we didn't want.

"I don't wish her no 'arm," ses the skipper, arter thinking for a long time. "Was that the fust letter you 'ad from 'er, Bill?"

"Fust and last," I ses, grinding my teeth.

"I hope they won't meet 'er, pore thing," he ses.

"I've been married longer than wot you have," I ses, "and I tell you one thing. It won't make no difference to us whether they do or they don't," I ses.

And it didn't.

THE VIGIL

"I'm the happiest man in the world," said Mr. Farrer, in accents of dreamy tenderness.

Miss Ward sighed. "Wait till father comes in," she said.

Mr. Farrer peered through the plants which formed a welcome screen to the window and listened with some uneasiness. He was waiting for the firm, springy step that should herald the approach of ex-Sergeant-Major Ward. A squeeze of Miss Ward's hand renewed his courage.

"Perhaps I had better light the lamp," said the girl, after a long pause. "I wonder where mother's got to?"

"She's on my side, at any rate," said Mr. Farrer.

"Poor mother!" said the girl. "She daren't call her soul her own. I expect she's sitting in her bedroom with the door shut. She hates unpleasantness. And there's sure to be some."

"So do I," said the young man, with a slight shiver. "But why should there be any? He doesn't want you to keep single all your life, does he?"

"He'd like me to marry a soldier," said Miss Ward. "He says that the young men of the present day are too soft. The only thing he thinks about is courage and strength."

She rose and, placing the lamp on the table, removed the chimney, and then sought round the room for the matches. Mr. Farrer, who had two boxes in his pocket, helped her.

They found a box at last on the mantelpiece, and Mr. Farrer steadied her by placing one arm round her waist while she lit the lamp. A sudden exclamation from outside reminded them that the blind was not yet drawn, and they sprang apart in dismay as a grizzled and upright old warrior burst into the room and confronted them.

"Pull that blind down!" he roared. "Not you," he continued, as Mr. Farrer hastened to help. "What do you mean by touching my blind? What do you mean by embracing my daughter? Eh? Why don't you answer?"

"We—we are going to be married," said Mr. Farrer, trying to speak boldly.

The sergeant-major drew himself up, and the young man gazed in dismay at a chest which seemed as though it would never cease expanding.

"Married!" exclaimed the sergeant-major, with a grim laugh. "Married to a little tame bunny-rabbit! Not if I know it. Where's your mother?" he demanded, turning to the girl.

"Upstairs," was the reply.

Her father raised his voice, and a nervous reply came from above. A minute later Mrs. Ward, pale of cheek, entered the room.

"Here's fine goings-on!" said the sergeant major, sharply. "I go for a little walk, and when I come back this—this infernal cockroach has got its arm round my daughter's waist. Why don't you look after her? Do you know anything about it?"

His wife shook her head.

"Five feet four and about thirty round the chest, and wants to marry my daughter!" said the sergeant-major, with a sneer. "Eh? What's that? What did you say? What?"

"I said that's a pretty good size for a cockroach," murmured Mr. Farrer, defiantly. "Besides, size isn't everything. If it was, you'd be a general instead of only a sergeant-major."

"You get out of my house," said the other, as soon as he could get his breath. "Go on Sharp with it."

"I'm going," said the mortified Mr. Farrer. "I'm sorry if I was rude. I came on purpose to see you to-night. Bertha—Miss Ward, I mean—told me your ideas, but I couldn't believe her. I said you'd got more common sense than to object to a man just because he wasn't a soldier."

"I want a man for a son-in-law," said the other. "I don't say he's got to be a soldier."

"Just so," said Mr. Farrer. "You're a man, ain't you? Well, I'll do anything that you'll do."

"Pph!" said the sergeant-major. "I've done my little lot. I've been in action four times, and wounded in three places. That's my tally."

"The colonel said once that my husband doesn't know what fear is," said Mrs. Ward, timidly. "He's afraid of nothing."

"Except ghosts," remarked her daughter, softly.

"Hold your tongue, miss," said her father, twisting his moustache. "No sensible man is afraid of what doesn't exist."

"A lot of people believe they do, though," said Mr. Farrer, breaking in. "I heard the other night that old Smith's ghost has been seen again swinging from the apple tree. Three people have seen it."

"Rubbish!" said the sergeant-major.

"Maybe," said the young man; "but I'll bet you, Mr. Ward, for all your courage, that you won't go up there alone at twelve o'clock one night to see."

"I thought I ordered you out of my house just now," said the sergeant-major, glaring at him.

"Going into action," said Mr. Farrer, pausing at the door, "is one thing —you have to obey orders and you can't help yourself; but going to a lonely cottage two miles off to see the ghost of a man that hanged himself is another."

"Do you mean to say I'm afraid?" blustered the other.

Mr. Farrer shook his head. "I don't say anything," he remarked; "but even a cockroach does a bit of thinking sometimes."

"Perhaps you'd like to go," said the sergeant-major.

"I don't mind," said the young man; "and perhaps you'll think a little better of me, Mr. Ward. If I do what you're afraid to do—"

Mrs. Ward and her daughter flung themselves hastily between the sergeant-major and his intended sacrifice. Mr. Farrer, pale but determined, stood his ground.

"I'll dare you to go up and spend a night there alone," he said.

"I'll dare you," said the incensed warrior, weakly.

"All right; I'll spend Wednesday night there," said Mr. Farrer, "and I'll come round on Thursday and let you know how I got on."

"I dare say," said the other; "but I don't want you here, and, what's more, I won't have you. You can go to Smith's cottage on Wednesday at twelve o'clock if you like, and I'll go up any time between twelve and three and make sure you're there. D'ye understand? I'll show you whether I'm afraid or not."

"There's no reason for you to be afraid," said Mr. Farrer. "I shall be there to protect you. That's very different to being there alone, as I shall be. But, of course, you can go up the next night by yourself, and wait for me, if you like. If you like to prove your courage, I mean."

"When I want to be ordered about," said the sergeant-major, in a magnificent voice, "I'll let you know. Now go, before I do anything I might be sorry for afterwards."

He stood at the door, erect as a ramrod, and watched the young man up the road. His conversation at the supper-table that night related almost entirely to puppy-dogs and the best way of training them.

He kept a close eye upon his daughter for the next day or two, but human nature has its limits. He tried to sleep one afternoon in his easy-chair with one eye open, but the exquisite silence maintained by Miss Ward was too much for it. A hum of perfect content arose from the feature below, and five minutes later Miss Ward was speeding in search of Mr. Farrer.

"I had to come, Ted," she said, breathlessly, "because to-morrow's Wednesday. I've got something to tell you, but I don't know whether I ought to."

"Tell me and let me decide," said Mr. Farrer, tenderly.

"I—I'm so afraid you might be frightened," said the girl. "I won't tell you, but I'll give you a hint. If you see anything awful, don't be frightened."

Mr. Farrer stroked her hand. "The only thing I'm afraid of is your father," he said, softly.

"Oh!" said the girl, clasping her hands together. "You have guessed it."

"Guessed it?" said Mr. Farrer.

Miss Ward nodded. "I happened to pass his door this morning," she said, in a low voice. "It was open a little way, and he was standing up and measuring one of mother's nightgowns against his chest. I couldn't think what he was doing it for at first."

Mr. Farrer whistled and his face hardened.

"That's not fair play," he said at last. "All right; I'll be ready for him."

"He doesn't like to be put in the wrong," said Miss Ward. "He wants to prove that you haven't got any courage. He'd be disappointed if he found you had."

"All right," said Mr. Farrer again. "You're an angel for coming to tell me."

"Father would call me something else, I expect," said Miss Ward, with a smile. "Good-bye. I want to get back before he wakes up."

She was back in her chair, listening to her father's slumbers, half an hour before he awoke.

"I'm making up for to-morrow night," he said, opening his eyes suddenly.

His daughter nodded.

"Shows strength of will," continued the sergeant-major, amiably. "Wellington could go to sleep at any time by just willing it. I'm the same way; I can go to sleep at five minutes' notice."

"It's a very useful gift," said Miss Ward, piously, "very."

Mr. Ward had two naps the next day. He awoke from the second at twelve-thirty a.m., and in a somewhat disagreeable frame of mind rose and stretched himself. The house was very still. He took a small brown-paper parcel from behind the sofa and, extinguishing the lamp, put on his cap and opened the front door.

If the house was quiet, the little street seemed dead. He closed the door softly and stepped into the darkness. In terms which would have been understood by "our army in Flanders" he execrated the forefathers, the name, and the upbringing of Mr. Edward Farrer.

Not a soul in the streets; not a light in a window. He left the little town behind, passed the last isolated house on the road, and walked into the greater blackness of a road between tall hedges. He had put on canvas shoes with rubber soles, for the better surprise of Mr. Farrer, and his own progress seemed to partake of a ghostly nature. Every ghost story he had ever heard or read crowded into his memory. For the first time in his experience even the idea of the company of Mr. Farrer seemed better than no company at all.

The night was so dark that he nearly missed the turning that led to the cottage. For the first few yards he had almost to feel his way; then, with a greater yearning than ever for the society of Mr. Farrer, he straightened his back and marched swiftly and noiselessly towards the cottage.

It was a small, tumble-down place, set well back in an overgrown garden. The sergeant-major came to a halt just before reaching the gate, and, hidden by the hedge, unfastened his parcel and shook out his wife's best nightgown.

He got it over his head with some difficulty, and, with his arms in the sleeves, tried in vain to get his big hands through the small, lace-trimmed wristbands. Despite his utmost efforts he could only get two or three fingers through, and after a vain search for his cap, which had fallen off in the struggle, he made his way to the gate and stood there waiting. It was at this moment that the thought occurred to him that Mr. Farrer might have failed to keep the appointment.

His knees trembled slightly and he listened anxiously for any sound from the house. He rattled the gate and, standing with white arms outstretched, waited. Nothing happened. He shook it again, and then, pulling himself together, opened it and slipped into the garden. As he did so a large bough which lay in the centre of the footpath thoughtfully drew on one side to let him pass.

Mr. Ward stopped suddenly and, with his gaze fixed on the bough, watched it glide over the grass until it was swallowed up in the darkness. His own ideas of frightening Mr. Farrer were forgotten, and in a dry, choking voice he called loudly upon the name of that gentleman.

He called two or three times, with no response, and then, in a state of panic, backed slowly towards the gate with his eyes fixed on the house. A loud crash sounded from somewhere inside, the door was flung violently open, and a gruesome figure in white hopped out and squatted on the step.

It was evident to Sergeant-Major Ward that Mr. Farrer was not there, and that no useful purpose could be served by remaining. It was clear that the young man's courage had failed him, and, with grey head erect, elbows working like the sails of a windmill, and the ends of the nightgown streaming behind him, the sergeant-major bent his steps towards home.

He dropped into a walk after a time and looked carefully over his shoulder. So far as he could see he was alone, but the silence and loneliness were oppressive. He looked again, and, without stopping to inquire whether his eyes had deceived him, broke into a run again. Alternately walking and running, he got back to the town, and walked swiftly along the streets to his house. Police-Constable Burgess, who was approaching from the other direction, reached it at almost the same moment, and, turning on his lantern, stood gaping with astonishment. "Anything wrong?" he demanded.

"Wrong?" panted the sergeant-major, trying to put a little surprise and dignity into his voice. "No."

"I thought it was a lady walking in her sleep at first," said the constable. "A tall lady."

The sergeant-major suddenly became conscious of the nightgown. "I've been—for a little walk," he said, still breathing hard. "I felt a bit chilly—so I—put this on."

"Suits you, too," said the constable, stiffly. "But you Army men always was a bit dressy. Now if I put that on I should look ridikerlous."

The door opened before Mr. Ward could reply, and revealed, in the light of a bedroom candle, the astonished countenances of his wife and daughter.

"George!" exclaimed Mrs. Ward.

"Father!" said Miss Ward.

The sergeant-major tottered in and, gaining the front room, flung himself into his arm-chair. A stiff glass of whisky and water, handed him by his daughter, was swallowed at a gulp.

"Did you go?" inquired Mrs. Ward, clasping her hands.

The sergeant-major, fully conscious of the suspicions aroused by his disordered appearance, rallied his faculties. "Not likely," he said, with a short laugh. "After I got outside I knew it was no good going there to look for that young snippet. He'd no more think of going there than he would of flying. I walked a little way down the road—for exercise—and then strolled back."

"But—my nightgown?" said the wondering Mrs. Ward.

"Put it on to frighten the constable," said her husband.

He stood up and allowed her to help him pull it off. His face was flushed and his hair tousled, but the bright fierceness of his eye was unquenched. In submissive silence she followed him to bed.

He was up late next morning, and made but a poor breakfast. His after-dinner nap was disturbed, and tea was over before he had regained his wonted calm. An hour later the arrival of a dignified and reproachful Mr. Farrer set him blazing again.

"I have come to see you about last night," said Mr. Farrer, before the other could speak. "A joke's a joke, but when you said you would come I naturally expected you would keep your word."

"Keep my word?" repeated the sergeant-major, almost choking with wrath.

"I stayed there in that lonely cottage from twelve to three, as per agreement, waiting for you," said Mr. Farrer.

"You were not there," shouted the sergeant-major.

"How do you know?" inquired the other.

The sergeant-major looked round helplessly at his wife and daughter.

"Prove it," said Mr. Farrer, pushing his advantage. "You questioned my courage, and I stayed there three hours. Where were you?"

"You were not there," said the sergeant-major. "I know. You can't bluff me. You were afraid."

"I was there, and I'll swear it," said Mr. Farrer. "Still, there's no harm done. I'll go there again to-night, and I'll dare you to come for me?"

"Dare?" said the sergeant-major, choking. "Dare?"

"Dare," repeated the other; "and if you don't come this time I'll spread it all over Marcham. To-morrow night you can go there and wait for me. If you see what I saw—"

"Oh, Ted!" said Miss Ward, with a shiver. "Saw?" said the sergeant-major, starting. "Nothing harmful," said Mr. Farrer, calmly.

"As a matter of fact, it was very interesting."

"What was?" demanded the sergeant-major.

"It sounds rather silly, as a matter of fact," said Mr. Farrer, slowly. "Still, I did see a broken bough moving about the garden."

Mr. Ward regarded him open-mouthed.

"Anything else?" he inquired, in a husky voice.

"A figure in white," said Mr. Farrer, "with long waving arms, hopping about like a frog. I don't suppose you believe me, but if you come to-night perhaps you'll see it yourself. It's very interesting.

"Wer—weren't you frightened?" inquired the staring Mrs. Ward.

Mr. Farrer shook his head. "It would take more than that to frighten me," he said, simply. "I should be ashamed of myself to be afraid of a poor thing like that. It couldn't do me any harm."

"Did you see its face?" inquired Mrs. Ward, nervously.

Mr. Farrer shook his head.

"What sort of a body had it got?" said her daughter.

"So far as I could see, very good," said Mr. Farrer. "Very good figure —not tall, but well made."

An incredible suspicion that had been forming in the sergeant-major's mind began to take shape. "Did you see anything else?" he asked, sharply.

"One more," said Mr. Farrer, regarding him pleasantly. "One I call the Running Ghost."

"Run—" began the sergeant-major, and stopped suddenly.

"It came in at the front gate," pursued Mr. Farrer. "A tall, well-knit figure of martial bearing—much about your height, Mr. Ward—with a beautiful filmy white robe down to its knees—"

He broke off in mild surprise, and stood gazing at Miss Ward, who, with her handkerchief to her mouth, was rocking helplessly in her chair.

"Knees," he repeated, quietly. "It came slowly down the path, and half way to the house it stopped, and in a frightened sort of voice called out my name. I was surprised, naturally, but before I could get to it—to reassure it—"

"That'll do," said the sergeant-major, rising hastily and drawing himself up to his full height.

"You asked me," said Mr. Farrer, in an aggrieved voice.

"I know I did," said the sergeant-major, breathing heavily. "I know I did; but if I sit here listening to any more of your lies I shall be ill. The best thing you can do is to take that giggling girl out and give her a breath of fresh air. I have done with her."

WATCH-DOGS

"It's a'most the only enj'yment I've got left," said the oldest inhabitant, taking a long, slow draught of beer, "that and a pipe o' baccy. Neither of 'em wants chewing, and that's a great thing when you ain't got anything worth speaking about left to chew with."

He put his mug on the table and, ignoring the stillness of the summer air, sheltered the flame of a match between his cupped hands and conveyed it with infinite care to the bowl of his pipe. A dull but crafty old eye squinting down the stem assured itself that the tobacco was well alight before the match was thrown away.

"As I was a-saying, kindness to animals is all very well," he said to the wayfarer who sat opposite him in the shade of the "Cauliflower" elms; "but kindness to your feller-creeturs is more. The pint wot you give me is gone, but I'm just as thankful to you as if it wasn't."

He half closed his eyes and, gazing on to the fields beyond, fell into a reverie so deep that he failed to observe the landlord come for his mug and return with it filled. A little start attested his surprise, and, to his great annoyance, upset a couple of tablespoonfuls of the precious liquid.

"Some people waste all their kindness on dumb animals," he remarked, after the landlord had withdrawn from his offended vision, "but I was never a believer in it. I mind some time ago when a gen'lemen from Lunnon wot 'ad more money than sense offered a prize for kindness to animals. I was the only one that didn't try for to win it.

"Mr. Bunnett 'is name was, and 'e come down and took Farmer Hall's 'ouse for the summer. Over sixty 'e was, and old enough to know better. He used to put saucers of milk all round the 'ouse for cats to drink, and, by the time pore Farmer Hall got back, every cat for three miles round 'ad got in the habit of coming round to the back-door and asking for milk as if it was their right. Farmer Hall poisoned a saucer o' milk at last, and then 'ad to pay five shillings for a thin black cat with a mangy tail and one eye that Bob Pretty said belonged to 'is children. Farmer Hall said he'd go to jail afore he'd pay, at fust, but arter five men 'ad spoke the truth and said they 'ad see Bob's youngsters tying a empty mustard-tin to its tail on'y the day afore, he gave way.

"Tha was Bob Pretty all over, that was; the biggest raskel Claybury 'as ever had; and it wasn't the fust bit o' money 'e made out o' Mr. Bunnett coming to the place.

"It all come through Mr. Bunnett's love for animals. I never see a man so fond of animals as 'e was, and if he had 'ad 'is way Claybury would 'ave been overrun by 'em by this time. The day arter 'e got to the farm he couldn't eat 'is breakfuss because of a pig that was being killed in the yard, and it was no good pointing out to 'im that the pig was on'y making a fuss about it because it was its nature so to do. He lived on wegetables and such like, and the way 'e carried on one day over 'arf a biled caterpillar 'e found in his cabbage wouldn't be believed. He wouldn't eat another mossel, but sat hunting 'igh and low for the other 'arf.

"He 'adn't been in Claybury more than a week afore he said 'ow surprised 'e was to see 'ow pore dumb animals was treated. He made a little speech about it one evening up at the schoolroom, and, arter he 'ad finished, he up and offered to give a prize of a gold watch that used to belong to 'is dear sister wot loved animals, to the one wot was the kindest to 'em afore he left the place.

"If he'd ha' known Claybury men better 'e wouldn't ha' done it. The very next morning Bill Chambers took 'is baby's milk for the cat, and smacked 'is wife's 'ead for talking arter he'd told 'er to stop. Henery Walker got into trouble for leaning over Charlie Stubbs's fence and feeding his chickens for 'im, and Sam Jones's wife had to run off 'ome to 'er mother 'arf-dressed because she had 'appened to overlay a sick rabbit wot Sam 'ad taken to bed with 'im to keep warm.

"People used to stop animals in the road and try and do 'em a kindness— especially when Mr. Bunnett was passing—and Peter Gubbins walked past 'is house one day with ole Mrs. Broad's cat in 'is arms. A bad-tempered old cat it was, and, wot with Peter kissing the top of its 'ead and calling of it Tiddleums, it nearly went out of its mind.

"The fust time Mr. Bunnett see Bob Pretty was about a week arter he'd offered that gold watch. Bob was stooping down very careful over something in the hedge, and Mr. Bunnett, going up quiet-like behind 'im, see 'im messing about with a pore old toad he 'ad found, with a smashed leg.

"'Wots the matter with it?' ses Mr. Bunnett.

"Bob didn't seem to hear 'im. He was a-kneeling on the ground with 'is 'ead on one side looking at the toad; and by and by he pulled out 'is pocket'an'kercher and put the toad in it, as if it was made of egg-shells, and walked away.

"'Wot's the matter with it?' ses Mr. Bunnett, a'most trotting to keep up with 'im.

"'Got it's leg 'urt in some way, pore thing,' ses Bob. 'I want to get it 'ome as soon as I can and wash it and put it on a piece o' damp moss. But I'm afraid it's not long for this world.'

"Mr. Bunnett said it did 'im credit, and walked home alongside of 'im talking. He was surprised to find that Bob hadn't 'eard anything of the gold watch 'e was offering, but Bob said he was a busy, 'ard-working man and didn't 'ave no time to go to hear speeches or listen to tittle-tattle.

"'When I've done my day's work,' he ses, 'I can always find a job in the garden, and arter that I go in and 'elp my missis put the children to bed. She ain't strong, pore thing, and it's better than wasting time and money up at the "Cauliflower."'

"He 'ad a lot o' talk with Mr. Bunnett for the next day or two, and when 'e went round with the toad on the third day as lively and well as possible the old gen'leman said it was a miracle. And so it would ha' been if it had been the same toad.

"He took a great fancy to Bob Pretty, and somehow or other they was always dropping acrost each other. He met Bob with 'is dog one day—a large, ugly brute, but a'most as clever as wot Bob was 'imself. It stood there with its tongue 'anging out and looking at Bob uneasy-like out of the corner of its eye as Bob stood a-patting of it and calling it pet names.

"' Wunnerful affectionate old dog, ain't you, Joseph?' ses Bob.

"'He's got a kind eye,' ses Mr. Bunnett.

"'He's like another child to me, ain't you, my pretty?' ses Bob, smiling at 'im and feeling in 'is pocket. 'Here you are, old chap.'

"He threw down a biskit so sudden that Joseph, thinking it was a stone, went off like a streak o' lightning with 'is tail between 'is legs and yelping his 'ardest. Most men would ha' looked a bit foolish, but Bob Pretty didn't turn a hair.

"'Ain't it wunnerful the sense they've got,' he ses to Mr. Bunnett, wot was still staring arter the dog.

"'Sense?' ses the old gen'leman.

"'Yes,' ses Bob smiling. 'His food ain't been agreeing with 'im lately and he's starving hisself for a bit to get round agin, and 'e knew that 'e couldn't trust hisself alongside o' this biskit. Wot a pity men ain't like that with beer. I wish as 'ow Bill Chambers and Henery Walker and a few more 'ad been 'ere just now.'

"Mr. Bunnett agreed with 'im, and said wot a pity it was everybody 'adn't got Bob Pretty's commonsense and good feeling.

"'It ain't that,' ses Bob, shaking his 'ead at him; 'it ain't to my credit. I dessay if Sam Jones and Peter Gubbins, and Charlie Stubbs and Dicky Weed 'ad been brought up the same as I was they'd 'ave been a lot better than wot I am.'

"He bid Mr. Bunnett good-bye becos 'e said he'd got to get back to 'is work, and Mr. Bunnett had 'ardly got 'ome afore Henery Walker turned up full of anxiousness to ask his advice about five little baby kittens wot 'is old cat had found in the wash-place: the night afore.

"'Drownd them little innercent things, same as most would do, I can't,' he ses, shaking his 'ead; 'but wot to do with 'em I don't know.'

"'Couldn't you find 'omes for 'em?' ses Mr. Bunnett.

"Henery Walker shook his 'ead agin. ''Tain't no use thinking o' that,' he ses. 'There's more cats than 'omes about 'ere'. Why, Bill Chambers drownded six o'ny last week right afore the eyes of my pore little boy. Upset 'im dreadful it did.'

"Mr. Bunnett walked up and down the room thinking. 'We must try and find 'omes for 'em when they are old enough,' he says at last; 'I'll go round myself and see wot I can do for you.'

"Henery Walker thanked 'im and went off 'ome doing a bit o' thinking; and well he 'ad reason to. Everybody wanted one o' them kittens. Peter Gubbins offered for to take two, and Mr. Bunnett told Henery Walker next day that 'e could ha' found 'omes for 'em ten times over.

"'You've no idea wot fine, kind-'arted people they are in this village when their 'arts are touched,' he ses, smiling at Henery. 'You ought to 'ave seen Mr. Jones's smile when I asked 'im to take one. It did me good to see it. And I spoke to Mr. Chambers about drowning 'is kittens, and he told me 'e hadn't slept a wink ever since. And he offered to take your old cat to make up for it, if you was tired of keeping it.

"It was very 'ard on Henery Walker, I must say that. Other people was getting the credit of bringing up 'is kittens, and more than that, they used to ask Mr. Bunnett into their places to see 'ow the little dears was a-getting on.

"Kindness to animals caused more unpleasantness in Claybury than anything 'ad ever done afore. There was hardly a man as 'ud speak civil to each other, and the wimmen was a'most as bad. Cats and dogs and such-like began to act as if the place belonged to 'em, and seven people stopped Mr. Bunnett one day to tell 'im that Joe Parsons 'ad been putting down rat-poison and killed five little baby rats and their mother.

"It was some time afore anybody knew that Bob Pretty 'ad got 'is eye on that gold watch, and when they did they could 'ardly believe it. They give Bob credit for too much sense to waste time over wot they knew 'e couldn't get, but arter they 'ad heard one or two things they got alarmed, and pretty near the whole village went up to see Mr. Bunnett and tell 'im about Bob's true character. Mr. Bunnett couldn't believe 'em at fast, but arter they 'ad told 'im of Bob's poaching and the artful ways and tricks he 'ad of getting money as didn't belong to 'im 'e began to think different. He spoke to parson about 'im, and arter that 'e said he never wanted for to see Bob Pretty's face again.

"There was a fine to-do about it up at this 'ere Cauliflower public-'ouse that night, and the quietest man 'o the whole lot was Bob Pretty. He sat still all the time drinking 'is beer and smiling at 'em and giving 'em good advice 'ow to get that gold watch.

"'It's no good to me,' he ses, shaking his 'ead. 'I'm a pore labourin' man, and I know my place.'

"'Ow you could ever 'ave thought you 'ad a chance, Bob, I don't know,' ses Henery Walker.

"'Ow's the toad, Bob?' ses Bill Chambers; and then they all laughed.

"'Laugh away, mates,' ses Bob; 'I know you don't mean it. The on'y thing I'm sorry for is you can't all 'ave the gold watch, and I'm sure you've worked 'ard enough for it; keeping Henery Walker's kittens for 'im, and hanging round Mr. Bunnett's.'

"'We've all got a better chance than wot you 'ave, Bob,' ses little Dicky Weed the tailor.

"The quietest man o' the whole lot was Bob Pretty"

"'Ah, that's your iggernerance, Dicky,' ses Bob. 'Come to think it over quiet like, I'm afraid I shall win it arter all. Cos why? Cos I deserves it.'

"They all laughed agin, and Bill Chambers laughed so 'arty that 'e joggled Peter Gubbins's arm and upset 'is beer.

"'Laugh away,' ses Bob, pretending to get savage. 'Them that laughs best laughs last, mind. I'll 'ave that watch now, just to spite you all.'

"'Ow are you going to get it, Bob?' ses Sam Jones, jeering.

"'Never you mind, mate,' ses Bob, stamping 'is foot; 'I'm going to win it fair. I'm going to 'ave it for kindness to pore dumb animals.'

"'Ear! 'ear!' ses Dicky Weed, winking at the others. 'Will you 'ave a bet on it, Bob?'

"'No,' ses Bob Pretty; 'I don't want to win no man's money. I like to earn my money in the sweat o' my brow.'

"'But you won't win it, Bob,' ses Dicky, grinning. 'Look 'ere! I'll lay you a level bob you don't get it.'

"Bob shook his 'ead, and started talking to Bill Chambers about something else.

"'I'll bet you two bob to one, Bob,' ses Dicky. 'Well, three to one, then.'

"Bob sat up and looked at'im for a long time, considering, and at last he ses, 'All right,' he ses, 'if Smith the landlord will mind the money I will.'

"He 'anded over his shilling,' but very slow-like, and Dicky Weed 'anded over 'is money. Arter that Bob sat looking disagreeable like, especially when. Dicky said wot 'e was goin' to do with the money, and by an by Sam Jones dared 'im to 'ave the same bet with 'im in sixpences.

"Bob Pretty 'ad a pint more beer to think it over, and arter Bill Chambers 'ad stood 'im another, he said 'e would. He seemed a bit dazed like, and by the time he went 'ome he 'ad made bets with thirteen of 'em. Being Saturday night they 'ad all got money on 'em, and, as for Bob, he always 'ad some. Smith took care of the money and wrote it all up on a slate.

"'Why don't you 'ave a bit on, Mr. Smith?' ses Dicky.

"'Oh, I dunno,' ses Smith, wiping down the bar with a wet cloth.

"'It's the chance of a lifetime,' ses Dicky.

"'Looks like it,' ses Smith, coughing.

"'But 'e can't win,' ses Sam Jones, looking a bit upset. 'Why, Mr. Bunnett said 'e ought to be locked up.'

"'He's been led away,' ses Bob Pretty, shaking his 'ead. 'He's a kind-'arted old gen'leman when 'e's left alone, and he'll soon see wot a mistake 'e's made about me. I'll show 'im. But I wish it was something more useful than a gold watch.'

"'You ain't got it yet,' ses Bill Chambers.

"'No, mate,' ses Bob.

"'And you stand to lose a sight o' money,' ses Sam Jones. 'If you like, Bob Pretty, you can 'ave your bet back with me.'

"'Never mind, Sam,' ses Bob; 'I won't take no advantage of you. If I lose you'll 'ave sixpence to buy a rabbit-hutch with. Good-night, mates all.'

"He rumpled Bill Chambers's 'air for 'im as he passed—a thing Bill never can a-bear—and gave Henery Walker, wot was drinking beer, a smack on the back wot nearly ruined 'im for life.

"Some of 'em went and told Mr. Bunnett some more things about Bob next day, but they might as well ha' saved their breath. The old gen'leman said be knew all about 'im and he never wanted to 'ear his name mentioned agin. Arter which they began for to 'ave a more cheerful way of looking at things; and Sam Jones said 'e was going to 'ave a hole bored through 'is sixpence and wear it round 'is neck to aggravate Bob Pretty with.

"For the next three or four weeks Bob Pretty seemed to keep very quiet, and we all began to think as 'ow he 'ad made a mistake for once. Everybody else was trying their 'ardest for the watch, and all Bob done was to make a laugh of 'em and to say he believed it was on'y made of brass arter all. Then one arternoon, just a few days afore Mr. Bunnett's time was up at the farm, Bob took 'is dog out for a walk, and arter watching the farm for some time met the old gen'leman by accident up at Coe's plantation.

"'Good arternoon, sir,' he ses, smiling at 'im. 'Wot wunnerful fine weather we're a-having for the time o' year. I've just brought Joseph out for a bit of a walk. He ain't been wot I might call hisself for the last day or two, and I thought a little fresh air might do 'im good.'

"Mr. Bunnett just looked at him, and then 'e passed 'im by without a word.

"'I wanted to ask your advice about 'im,' ses Bob, turning round and follering of 'im. 'He's a delikit animal, and sometimes I wonder whether I 'aven't been a-pampering of 'im too much.'

"'Go away,' ses Mr. Bunnett; 'I've 'eard all about you. Go away at once.'

"'Heard all about me?' ses Bob Pretty, looking puzzled. 'Well, you can't 'ave heard no 'arm, that's one comfort.'

"'I've been told your true character,' ses the old gen'leman, very firm. 'And I'm ashamed that I should have let myself be deceived by you. I hope you'll try and do better while there is still time.'

"'If anybody 'as got anything to say agin my character,' says Bob, 'I wish as they'd say it to my face. I'm a pore, hard-working man, and my character's all I've got.'

"'You're poorer than you thought you was then,' says Mr. Bunnett. 'I wish you good arternoon.'

"'Good arternoon, sir,' ses Bob, very humble. 'I'm afraid some on 'em 'ave been telling lies about me, and I didn't think I'd got a enemy in the world. Come on, Joseph. Come on, old pal. We ain't wanted here.'

"He shook 'is 'ead with sorrow, and made a little sucking noise between 'is teeth, and afore you could wink, his dog 'ad laid hold of the old gen'leman's leg and kep' quiet waiting orders.

"'Help!' screams Mr. Bunnett. 'Call, 'im off! Call 'im off!'

"Bob said arterwards that 'e was foolish enough to lose 'is presence o' mind for a moment, and instead o' doing anything he stood there gaping with 'is mouth open.

"'Call 'im off!' screams Mr. Bunnett, trying to push the dog away. 'Why don't you call him off?'

"'Don't move,' ses Bob Pretty in a frightened voice. 'Don't move, wotever you do.'

"'Call him off! Take 'im away!' ses Mr. Bunnett.

"'Why, Joseph! Joseph! Wotever are you a-thinking of?' ses Bob, shaking 'is 'ead at the dog. 'I'm surprised at you! Don't you know Mr. Bunnett wot is so fond of animals?'

"'If you don't call 'im off, ses Mr. Bunnett, trembling all over, 'I'll have you locked up.'

"'I am a-calling 'im off,' ses Bob, looking very puzzled. 'Didn't you 'ear me? It's you making that noise that excites 'im, I think. P'r'aps if you keep quiet he'll leave go. Come off, Joseph, old boy, there's a good doggie. That ain't a bone.'

"'It's no good talking to 'im like that,' ses Mr. Bunnett, keeping quiet but trembling worse than ever. 'Make him let go.'

"'I don't want to 'urt his feelings,' ses Bob; 'they've got their feelings the same as wot we 'ave. Besides, p'r'aps it ain't 'is fault— p'r'aps he's gone mad.'

"'HELP!' ses the old gen'leman, in a voice that might ha' been heard a mile away. 'HELP!'

"'Why don't you keep quiet?' ses Bob. 'You're on'y frightening the pore animal and making things worse. Joseph, leave go and I'll see whether there's a biskit in my pocket. Why don't you leave go?'

"'Pull him off. Hit 'im,' ses Mr. Bunnett, shouting.

"'Wot?' ses Bob Pretty, with a start. 'Hit a poor, dumb animal wot don't know no better! Why, you'd never forgive me, sir, and I should lose the gold watch besides.'

"'No, you won't,' ses Mr. Bunnett, speaking very fast. 'You'll 'ave as much chance of it as ever you had. Hit 'im! Quick!'

"'It 'ud break my 'art,' ses Bob. 'He'd never forgive me; but if you'll take the responserbility, and then go straight 'ome and give me the gold watch now for kindness to animals, I will.'

"He shook his 'ead with sorrow and made that sucking noise agin.'

"'All right, you shall 'ave it,' ses Mr. Bunnett, shouting. 'You shall 'ave it.'

"'For kindness to animals?' ses Bob. 'Honour bright?'

"'Yes,' ses Mr. Bunnett.

"Bob Pretty lifted 'is foot and caught Joseph one behind that surprised 'im. Then he 'elped Mr. Bunnett look at 'is leg, and arter pointing out that the skin wasn't hardly broken, and saying that Joseph 'ad got the best mouth of any dog in Claybury, 'e walked 'ome with the old gen'leman and got the watch. He said Mr. Bunnett made a little speech when 'e gave it to 'im wot he couldn't remember, and wot he wouldn't repeat if 'e could.

"He came up to this 'ere Cauliflower public-'ouse the same night for the money 'e had won, and Bill Chambers made another speech, but, as Smith the landlord put' in outside for it, it didn't do Bob Pretty the good it ought to ha' done."

THE WEAKER VESSEL

Mr. Gribble sat in his small front parlour in a state of angry amazement. It was half-past six and there was no Mrs. Gribble; worse still, there was no tea. It was a state of things that had only happened once before. That was three weeks after marriage, and on that occasion Mr. Gribble had put his foot down with a bang that had echoed down the corridors of thirty years.

The fire in the little kitchen was out, and the untidy remains of Mrs. Gribble's midday meal still disgraced the table. More and more dazed, the indignant husband could only come to the conclusion that she had gone out and been run over. Other things might possibly account for her behaviour; that was the only one that would excuse it.

His meditations were interrupted by the sound of a key in the front door, and a second later a small, anxious figure entered the room and, leaning against the table, strove to get its breath. The process was not helped by the alarming distension of Mr. Gribble's figure.

"I—I got home—quick as I could—Henry," said Mrs. Gribble, panting.

"Where is my tea?" demanded her husband. "What do you mean by it? The fire's out and the kitchen is just as you left it."

"I—I've been to a lawyer's, Henry," said Mrs. Gribble, "and I had to wait."

"Lawyer's?" repeated her husband.

"I got a letter this afternoon telling me to call. Poor Uncle George, that went to America, is gone."

"That is no excuse for neglecting me," said Mr. Gribble. "Of course people die when they are old. Is that the one that got on and made money?"

His wife, apparently struggling to repress a little excitement, nodded. "He—he's left me two hundred pounds a year for life, Henry," she said, dabbing at her pale blue eyes with a handkerchief. "They're going to pay it monthly; sixteen pounds thirteen shillings and fourpence a month. That's how he left it."

"Two hund—" began Mr. Gribble, forgetting himself. "Two hun—Go and get my tea! If you think you're going to give yourself airs because your uncle's left you money, you won't do it in my house."

He took a chair by the window, and, while his wife busied herself in the kitchen, sat gazing in blank delight at the little street. Two hundred a year! It was all he could do to resume his wonted expression as his wife re-entered the room and began to lay the table. His manner, however, when she let a cup and saucer slip from her trembling fingers to smash on the floor left nothing to be desired.

"It's nice to have money come to us in our old age," said Mrs. Gribble, timidly, as they sat at tea. "It takes a load off my mind."

"Old age!" said her husband, disagreeably. "What d'ye mean by old age? I'm fifty-two, and feel as young as ever I did."

"You look as young as ever you did," said the docile Mrs. Gribble. "I can't see no change in you. At least, not to speak of."

"Not so much talk," said her husband. "When I want your opinion of my looks I'll ask you for it. When do you start getting this money?"

"Tuesday week; first of May," replied his wife. "The lawyers are going to send it by registered letter."

Mr. Gribble grunted.

"I shall be sorry to leave the house for some things," said his wife, looking round. "We've been here a good many years now, Henry."

"Leave the house!" repeated Mr. Gribble, putting down his tea-cup and staring at her.

"Leave the house! What are you talking about?"

"But we can't stay here, Henry," faltered Mrs. Gribble. "Not with all that money. They are building some beautiful houses in Charlton Grove now—bathroom, tiled hearths, and beautiful stained glass in the front door; and all for twenty-eight pounds a year."

"Wonderful!" said the other, with a mocking glint in his eye.

"And iron palings to the front garden, painted chocolate-colour picked out with blue," continued his wife, eyeing him wistfully.

Mr. Gribble struck the table a blow with his fist. "This house is good enough for me," he roared; "and what's good enough for me is good enough for you. You want to waste money on show; that's what you want. Stained glass and bow-windows! You want a bow-window to loll about in, do you? Shouldn't wonder if you don't want a servant-gal to do the work."

Mrs. Gribble flushed guiltily, and caught her breath.

"We're going to live as we've always lived," pursued Mr. Gribble. "Money ain't going to spoil me. I ain't going to put on no side just because I've come in for a little bit. If you had your way we should end up in the workhouse."

He filled his pipe and smoked thoughtfully, while Mrs. Gribble cleared away the tea-things and washed up. Pictures, good to look upon, formed in the smoke-pictures of a hale, hearty man walking along the primrose path arm-in-arm with two hundred a year; of the mahogany and plush of the saloon bar at the Grafton Arms; of Sunday jaunts, and the Oval on summer afternoons.

He ate his breakfast slowly on the first of the month, and, the meal finished, took a seat in the window with his pipe and waited for the postman. Mrs. Gribble's timid reminders concerning the flight of time and consequent fines for lateness at work fell on deaf ears. He jumped up suddenly and met the postman at the door.

"Has it come?" inquired Mrs. Gribble, extending her hand.

By way of reply her husband tore open the envelope and, handing her the covering letter, counted the notes and coin and placed them slowly in his pockets. Then, as Mrs. Gribble looked at him, he looked at the clock, and, snatching up his hat, set off down the road.

He was late home that evening, and his manner forbade conversation. Mrs. Gribble, with the bereaved air of one who has sustained an irremediable loss, sighed fitfully, and once applied her handkerchief to her eyes.

"That's no good," said her husband at last; "that won't bring him back."

"Bring who back?" inquired Mrs. Gribble, in genuine surprise.

"Why, your Uncle George," said Mr. Gribble. "That's what you're turning on the water-cart for, ain't it?"

"I wasn't thinking of him," said Mrs. Gribble, trying to speak bravely. "I was thinking of—"

"Well, you ought to be," interrupted her husband. "He wasn't my uncle, poor chap, but I've been thinking of him, off and on, all day. That bloater-paste you are eating now came from his kindness. I brought it home as a treat."

"I was thinking of my clothes," said Mrs. Gribble, clenching her hands together under the table. "When I found I had come in for that money, the first thing I thought was that I should be able to have a decent dress. My old ones are quite worn out, and as for my hat and jacket—"

"Go on," said her husband, fiercely. "Go on. That's just what I said: trust you with money, and we should be poorer than ever."

"I'm ashamed to be seen out," said Mrs. Gribble.

"A woman's place is the home," said Mr. Gribble; "and so long as I'm satisfied with your appearance nobody else matters. So long as I am pleased, that's everything. What do you want to go dressing yourself up for? Nothing looks worse than an over-dressed woman."

"What are we going to do with all that money, then?" inquired Mrs. Gribble, in trembling tones.

"That'll do," said Mr. Gribble, decidedly. "That'll do. One o' these days you'll go too far. You start throwing that money in my teeth and see what happens. I've done my best for you all these years, and there's no reason to suppose I sha'n't go on doing so. What did you say? What!"

Mrs. Gribble turned to him a face rendered ghastly by terror. "I—I said—it was my money," she stammered.

Mr. Gribble rose, and stood for a full minute regarding her. Then, kicking a chair out of his way, he took his hat from its peg in the passage and, with a bang of the street-door that sent a current of fresh, sweet air circulating through the house, strode off to the Grafton Arms.

It was past eleven when he returned, but even the spectacle of his wife laboriously darning her old dress failed to reduce his good-humour in the slightest degree. In a frivolous mood he even took a feather from the dismembered hat on the table and stuck it in his hair. He took the stump of a strong cigar from his lips and, exhaling a final cloud of smoke, tossed it into the fireplace.

"Uncle George dead," he said, at last, shaking his head. "Hadn't pleasure acquaintance, but good man. Good man."

He shook his head again and gazed mistily at his wife.

"He was a teetotaller," she remarked, casually.

"He was tee-toiler," repeated Mr. Gribble, regarding her equably. "Good man. Uncle George dead-tee-toller."

Mrs. Gribble gathered up her work and began to put it away.

"Bed-time," said Mr. Gribble, and led the way upstairs, singing.

His good-humour had evaporated by the morning, and, having made a light breakfast of five cups of tea, he went off, with lagging steps, to work. It was a beautiful spring morning, and the idea of a man with two hundred a year and a headache going off to a warehouse instead of a day's outing seemed to border upon the absurd. What use was money without freedom? His toil was sweetened that day by the knowledge that he could drop it any time he liked and walk out, a free man, into the sunlight.

By the end of a week his mind was made up. Each day that passed made his hurried uprising and scrambled breakfast more and more irksome; and on Monday morning, with hands in trouser-pockets and legs stretched out, he leaned back in his chair and received his wife's alarming intimations as to the flight of time with a superior and sphinx-like smile.

"It's too fine to go to work to-day," he said, lazily. "Come to that, any day is too fine to waste at work."

Mrs. Gribble sat gasping at him.

"So on Saturday I gave 'em a week's notice," continued her husband, "and after Potts and Co. had listened while I told 'em what I thought of 'em, they said they'd do without the week's notice."

"You've never given up your job?" said Mrs. Gribble.

"I spoke to old Potts as one gentleman of independent means to another," said Mr. Gribble, smiling. "Thirty-five bob a week after twenty years' service! And he had the cheek to tell me I wasn't worth that. When I told him what he was worth he talked about sending for the police. What are you looking like that for? I've worked hard for you for thirty years, and I've had enough of it. Now it's your turn."

"You'd find it hard to get another place at your age," said his wife; "especially if they wouldn't give you a good character."

"Place!" said the other, staring. "Place! I tell you I've done with work. For a man o' my means to go on working for thirty-five bob a week is ridiculous."

"But suppose anything happened to me," said his wife, in a troubled voice.

"That's not very likely," said Mr. Gribble.

"You're tough enough. And if it did your money would come to me."

Mrs. Gribble shook her head.

"WHAT?" roared her husband, jumping up.

"I've only got it for life, Henry, as I told you," said Mrs. Gribble, in alarm. "I thought you knew it would stop when I died."

"And what's to become of me if anything happens to you, then?" demanded the dismayed Mr. Gribble. "What am I to do?"

Mrs. Gribble put her handkerchief to her eyes.

"And don't start weakening your constitution by crying," shouted the incensed husband.

"What are you mumbling?"

"I sa—sa—said, let's hope—you'll go first," sobbed his wife. "Then it will be all right."

Mr. Gribble opened his mouth, and then, realizing the inadequacy of the English language for moments of stress, closed it again. He broke his silence at last in favour of Uncle George.

"Mind you," he said, concluding a peroration which his wife listened to with her fingers in her ears— "mind you, I reckon I've been absolutely done by you and your precious Uncle George. I've given up a good situation, and now, any time you fancy to go off the hooks, I'm to be turned into the street."

"I'll try and live, for your sake, Henry," said his wife.

"Think of my worry every time you are ill," pursued the indignant Mr. Gribble.

Mrs. Gribble sighed, and her husband, after a few further remarks concerning Uncle George, his past and his future, announced his intention of going to the lawyers and seeing whether anything could be done. He came back in a state of voiceless gloom, and spent the rest of a beautiful day indoors, smoking a pipe which had lost much of its flavour, and regarding with a critical and anxious eye the small, weedy figure of his wife as she went about her work.

The second month's payment went into his pocket as a matter of course, but on this occasion Mrs. Gribble made no requests for new clothes or change of residence. A little nervous cough was her sole comment.

"Got a cold?" inquired her husband, starting.

"I don't think so," replied his wife, and, surprised and touched at this unusual display of interest, coughed again.

"Is it your throat or your chest?" he inquired, gruffly.

Mrs. Gribble coughed again to see. After five coughs she said she thought it was her chest.

"You'd better not go out o' doors to-day, then," said Mr. Gribble. "Don't stand about in draughts; and I'll fetch you in a bottle of cough mixture when I go out. What about a lay-down on the sofa?"

His wife thanked him, and, reaching the sofa, watched with half-closed eyes as he cleared the breakfast-table. It was the first time he had done such a thing in his life, and a little honest pride in the possession of such a cough would not be denied. Dim possibilities of its vast usefulness suddenly occurred to her.

She took the cough mixture for a week, by which time other symptoms, extremely disquieting to an ease-loving man, had manifested themselves. Going upstairs deprived her of breath; carrying a loaded tea-tray produced a long and alarming stitch in the side. The last time she ever filled the coal-scuttle she was discovered sitting beside it on the floor in a state of collapse.

"You'd better go and see the doctor," said Mr. Gribble.

Mrs. Gribble went. Years before the doctor had told her that she ought to take life easier, and she was now able to tell him she was prepared to take his advice.

"And, you see, I must take care of myself now for the sake of my husband," she said, after she had explained matters.

"I understand," said the doctor.

"If anything happened to me—" began the patient.

"Nothing shall happen," said the other. "Stay in bed to-morrow morning, and I'll come round and overhaul you."

Mrs. Gribble hesitated. "You might examine me and think I was all right," she objected; "and at the same time you wouldn't know how I feel."

"I know just how you feel," was the reply. "Good-bye."

He came round the following morning and, following the dejected Mr. Gribble upstairs, made a long and thorough investigation of his patient.

"Say 'ninety-nine,'" he said, adjusting his stethoscope.

Mrs. Gribble ticked off "ninety-nines" until her husband's ears ached with them. The doctor finished at last, and, fastening his bag, stood with his beard in his hand, pondering. He looked from the little, whitefaced woman on the bed to the bulky figure of Mr. Gribble.

"You had better lie up for a week," he said, decidedly. "The rest will do you good."

"Nothing serious, I s'pose?" said Mr. Gribble, as he led the way downstairs to the small parlour.

"She ought to be all right with care," was the reply.

"Care?" repeated the other, distastefully. "What's the matter with her?"

"She's not very strong," said the doctor; "and hearts don't improve with age, you know. Under favourable conditions she's good for some years yet. The great thing is never to thwart her. Let her have her own way in everything."

"Own way in everything?" repeated the dumbfounded Mr. Gribble.

The doctor nodded. "Never let her worry about anything," he continued; "and, above all, never find fault with her."

"Not," said Mr. Gribble, thickly—"not even for her own good?"

"Unless you want to run the risk of losing her."

Mr. Gribble shivered.

"Let her have an easy time," said the doctor, taking up his hat. "Pamper her a bit if you like; it won't hurt her. Above all, don't let that heart of hers get excited."

He shook hands with the petrified Mr. Gribble and went off, grinning wickedly. He had few favourites, and Mr. Gribble was not one of them.

For two days the devoted husband did the housework and waited on the invalid. Then he wearied, and, at his wife's suggestion, a small girl was engaged as servant. She did most of the nursing as well, and, having a great love for the sensational, took a grave view of her mistress's condition.

It was a relief to Mr. Gribble when his wife came downstairs again, and he was cheered to see that she looked much better. His satisfaction was so marked that it brought on her cough again.

"It's this house, I think," she said, with a resigned smile. "It never did agree with me."

"Well, you've lived in it a good many years," said her husband, controlling himself with difficulty.

"It's rather dark and small," said Mrs. Gribble. "Not but what it is good enough for me. And I dare say it will last my time."

"Nonsense!" said her husband, gruffly. "You want to get out a bit more. You've got nothing to do now we are wasting all this money on a servant. Why don't you go out for little walks?"

Mrs. Gribble went, after several promptings, and the fruit of one of them was handed by the postman to Mr. Gribble a few days afterwards. Half-choking with wrath and astonishment, he stood over his trembling wife with the first draper's bill he had ever received.

"One pound two shillings and threepence three-farthings!" he recited. "It must be a mistake. It must be for somebody else."

Mrs. Gribble, with her hand to her heart, tottered to the sofa and lay there with her eyes closed.

"I had to get some dress material," she said, in a quavering voice. "You want me to go out, and I'm so shabby I'm ashamed to be seen."

Mr. Gribble made muffled noises in his throat; then, afraid to trust himself, he went into the back-yard and, taking a seat on an upturned bucket, sat with his head in his hands peering into the future.

The dressmaker's bill and a bill for a new hat came after the next monthly payment; and a bill for shoes came a week later. Hoping much from the well-known curative effects of fine feathers, he managed to treat the affair with dignified silence. The only time he allowed full play to his feelings Mrs. Gribble took to her bed for two days, and the doctor had a heart-to-heart talk with him on the doorstep.

It was a matter of great annoyance to him that his wife still continued to attribute her ill-health to the smallness and darkness of the house; and the fact that there were only two of the houses in Charlton Grove left caused a marked depression of spirits. It was clear that she was fretting. The small servant went further, and said that she was fading away.

They moved at the September quarter, and a slight, but temporary, improvement in Mrs. Gribble's health took place. Her cheeks flushed and her eyes sparkled over new curtains and new linoleum. The tiled hearths, and stained glass in the front door filled her with a deep and solemn thankfulness. The only thing that disturbed her was the fact that Mr. Gribble, to avoid wasting money over necessaries, contrived to spend an unduly large portion on personal luxuries.

"We ought to have some new things for the kitchen," she said one day.

"No money," said Mr. Gribble, laconically.

"And a mat for the bathroom."

Mr. Gribble got up and went out.

She had to go to him for everything. Two hundred a year and not a penny she could call her own! She consulted her heart, and that faithful organ responded with a bound that set her nerves quivering. If she could only screw her courage to the sticking-point the question would be settled for once and all.

White and trembling she sat at breakfast on the first of November, waiting for the postman, while the unconscious Mr. Gribble went on with his meal. The double-knocks down the road came nearer and nearer, and Mr. Gribble, wiping his mouth, sat upright with an air of alert and pleased interest. Rapid steps came to the front door, and a double bang followed.

"Always punctual," said Mr. Gribble, good-humouredly.

His wife made no reply, but, taking a blue-crossed envelope from the maid in her shaking fingers, looked round for a knife. Her gaze encountered Mr. Gribble's outstretched hand.

"After you," he said sharply.

Mrs. Gribble found the knife, and, hacking tremulously at the envelope, peeped inside it and, with her gaze fastened on the window, fumbled for her pocket. She was so pale and shook so much that the words died away on her husband's lips.

"You—you had better let me take care of that," he said, at last.

"It is—all right," gasped his wife.

She put her hand to her throat and, hardly able to believe in her victory, sat struggling for breath. Before her, grim and upright, her husband sat, a figure of helpless smouldering wrath.

"You might lose it," he said, at last. "I sha'n't lose it," said his wife.

To avoid further argument, she arose and went slowly upstairs. Through the doorway Mr. Gribble saw her helping herself up by the banisters, her left hand still at her throat. Then he heard her moving slowly about in the bedroom overhead.

He took out his pipe and filled it mechanically, and was just holding a match to the tobacco when he paused and gazed with a puzzled air at the ceiling. "Blamed if it don't sound like somebody dancing!" he growled.

I.

Two men stood in the billiard-room of an old country house, talking. Play, which had been of a half-hearted nature, was over, and they sat at the open window, looking out over the park stretching away beneath them, conversing idly.

"Your time's nearly up, Jem," said one at length, "this time six weeks you'll be yawning out the honeymoon and cursing the man—woman I mean— who invented them."

Jem Benson stretched his long limbs in the chair and grunted in dissent.

"I've never understood it," continued Wilfred Carr, yawning. "It's not in my line at all; I never had enough money for my own wants, let alone for two. Perhaps if I were as rich as you or Croesus I might regard it differently."

There was just sufficient meaning in the latter part of the remark for his cousin to forbear to reply to it. He continued to gaze out of the window and to smoke slowly.

"Not being as rich as Croesus—or you," resumed Carr, regarding him from beneath lowered lids, "I paddle my own canoe down the stream of Time, and, tying it to my friends' door-posts, go in to eat their dinners."

"Quite Venetian," said Jem Benson, still looking out of the window. "It's not a bad thing for you, Wilfred, that you have the doorposts and dinners—and friends."

Carr grunted in his turn. "Seriously though, Jem," he said, slowly, "you're a lucky fellow, a very lucky fellow. If there is a better girl above ground than Olive, I should like to see her."

"Yes," said the other, quietly.

"She's such an exceptional girl," continued Carr, staring out of the window. "She's so good and gentle. She thinks you are a bundle of all the virtues."

He laughed frankly and joyously, but the other man did not join him. "Strong sense—of right and wrong, though," continued Carr, musingly. "Do you know, I believe that if she found out that you were not—"

"Not what?" demanded Benson, turning upon him fiercely, "Not what?"

"Everything that you are," returned his cousin, with a grin that belied his words, "I believe she'd drop you."

"Talk about something else," said Benson, slowly; "your pleasantries are not always in the best taste."

Wilfred Carr rose and taking a cue from the rack, bent over the board and practiced one or two favourite shots. "The only other subject I can talk about just at present is my own financial affairs," he said slowly, as he walked round the table.

"Talk about something else," said Benson again, bluntly.

"And the two things are connected," said Carr, and dropping his cue he half sat on the table and eyed his cousin.

There was a long silence. Benson pitched the end of his cigar out of the window, and leaning back closed his eyes.

"Do you follow me?" inquired Carr at length.

Benson opened his eyes and nodded at the window.

"Do you want to follow my cigar?" he demanded.

"I should prefer to depart by the usual way for your sake," returned the other, unabashed. "If I left by the window all sorts of questions would be asked, and you know what a talkative chap I am."

"So long as you don't talk about my affairs," returned the other, restraining himself by an obvious effort, "you can talk yourself hoarse."

"I'm in a mess," said Carr, slowly, "a devil of a mess. If I don't raise fifteen hundred by this day fortnight, I may be getting my board and lodging free."

"Would that be any change?" questioned Benson.

"The quality would," retorted the other. "The address also would not be good. Seriously, Jem, will you let me have the fifteen hundred?"

"No," said the other, simply.

Carr went white. "It's to save me from ruin," he said, thickly.

"I've helped you till I'm tired," said Benson, turning and regarding him, "and it is all to no good. If you've got into a mess, get out of it. You should not be so fond of giving autographs away."

"It's foolish, I admit," said Carr, deliberately. "I won't do so any more. By the way, I've got some to sell. You needn't sneer. They're not my own."

"Whose are they?" inquired the other.

"Yours."

Benson got up from his chair and crossed over to him. "What is this?" he asked, quietly. "Blackmail?"

"Call it what you like," said Carr. "I've got some letters for sale, price fifteen hundred. And I know a man who would buy them at that price for the mere chance of getting Olive from you. I'll give you first offer."

"If you have got any letters bearing my signature, you will be good enough to give them to me," said Benson, very slowly.

"They're mine," said Carr, lightly; "given to me by the lady you wrote them to. I must say that they are not all in the best possible taste."

His cousin reached forward suddenly, and catching him by the collar of his coat pinned him down on the table.

"Give me those letters," he breathed, sticking his face close to Carr's.

"They're not here," said Carr, struggling. "I'm not a fool. Let me go, or I'll raise the price."

The other man raised him from the table in his powerful hands, apparently with the intention of dashing his head against it. Then suddenly his hold relaxed as an astonished-looking maid-servant entered the room with letters. Carr sat up hastily.

"That's how it was done," said Benson, for the girl's benefit as he took the letters.

"I don't wonder at the other man making him pay for it, then," said Carr, blandly.

"You will give me those letters?" said Benson, suggestively, as the girl left the room.

"At the price I mentioned, yes," said Carr; "but so sure as I am a living man, if you lay your clumsy hands on me again, I'll double it. Now, I'll leave you for a time while you think it over."

He took a cigar from the box and lighting it carefully quitted the room. His cousin waited until the door had closed behind him, and then turning to the window sat there in a fit of fury as silent as it was terrible.

The air was fresh and sweet from the park, heavy with the scent of new-mown grass. The fragrance of a cigar was now added to it, and glancing out he saw his cousin pacing slowly by. He rose and went to the door, and then, apparently altering his mind, he returned to the window and watched the figure of his cousin as it moved slowly away into the moonlight. Then he rose again, and, for a long time, the room was empty.

It was empty when Mrs. Benson came in some time later to say good-night to her son on her way to bed. She walked slowly round the table, and pausing at the window gazed from it in idle thought, until she saw the figure of her son advancing with rapid strides toward the house. He looked up at the window.

"Good-night," said she.

"Good-night," said Benson, in a deep voice.

"Where is Wilfred?"

"Oh, he has gone," said Benson.

"Gone?"

"We had a few words; he was wanting money again, and I gave him a piece of my mind. I don't think we shall see him again."

"Poor Wilfred!" sighed Mrs. Benson. "He is always in trouble of some sort. I hope that you were not too hard upon him."

"No more than he deserved," said her son, sternly. "Good night."

II.

The well, which had long ago fallen into disuse, was almost hidden by the thick tangle of undergrowth which ran riot at that corner of the old park. It was partly covered by the shrunken half of a lid, above which a rusty windlass creaked in company with the music of the pines when the wind blew strongly. The full light of the sun never reached it, and the ground surrounding it was moist and green when other parts of the park were gaping with the heat.

Two people walking slowly round the park in the fragrant stillness of a summer evening strayed in the direction of the well.

"No use going through this wilderness, Olive," said Benson, pausing on the outskirts of the pines and eyeing with some disfavour the gloom beyond.

"Best part of the park," said the girl briskly; "you know it's my favourite spot."

"I know you're very fond of sitting on the coping," said the man slowly, "and I wish you wouldn't. One day you will lean back too far and fall in."

"And make the acquaintance of Truth," said Olive lightly. "Come along."

She ran from him and was lost in the shadow of the pines, the bracken crackling beneath her feet as she ran. Her companion followed slowly, and emerging from the gloom saw her poised daintily on the edge of the well with her feet hidden in the rank grass and nettles which surrounded it. She motioned her companion to take a seat by her side, and smiled softly as she felt a strong arm passed about her waist.

"I like this place," said she, breaking a long silence, "it is so dismal —so uncanny. Do you know I wouldn't dare to sit here alone, Jem. I should imagine that all sorts of dreadful things were hidden behind the bushes and trees, waiting to spring out on me. Ugh!"

"You'd better let me take you in," said her companion tenderly; "the well isn't always wholesome, especially in the hot weather.

"Let's make a move."

The girl gave an obstinate little shake, and settled herself more securely on her seat.

"Smoke your cigar in peace," she said quietly. "I am settled here for a quiet talk. Has anything been heard of Wilfred yet?"

"Nothing."

"Quite a dramatic disappearance, isn't it?" she continued. "Another scrape, I suppose, and another letter for you in the same old strain; 'Dear Jem, help me out.'"

Jem Benson blew a cloud of fragrant smoke into the air, and holding his cigar between his teeth brushed away the ash from his coat sleeves.

"I wonder what he would have done without you," said the girl, pressing his arm affectionately. "Gone under long ago, I suppose. When we are married, Jem, I shall presume upon the relationship to lecture him. He is very wild, but he has his good points, poor fellow."

"I never saw them," said Benson, with startling bitterness. "God knows I never saw them."

"He is nobody's enemy but his own," said the girl, startled by this outburst.

"You don't know much about him," said the other, sharply. "He was not above blackmail; not above ruining the life of a friend to do himself a benefit. A loafer, a cur, and a liar!"

The girl looked up at him soberly but timidly and took his arm without a word, and they both sat silent while evening deepened into night and the beams of the moon, filtering through the branches, surrounded them with a silver network. Her head sank upon his shoulder, till suddenly with a sharp cry she sprang to her feet.

"What was that?" she cried breathlessly.

"What was what?" demanded Benson, springing up and clutching her fast by the arm.

She caught her breath and tried to laugh.

"You're hurting me, Jem."

His hold relaxed.

"What is the matter?" he asked gently.

"What was it startled you?"

"I was startled," she said, slowly, putting her hands on his shoulder. "I suppose the words I used just now are ringing in my ears, but I fancied that somebody behind us whispered 'Jem, help me out.'"

"Fancy," repeated Benson, and his voice shook; "but these fancies are not good for you. You—are frightened—at the dark and the gloom of these trees. Let me take you back to the house."

"No, I'm not frightened," said the girl, reseating herself. "I should never be really frightened of anything when you were with me, Jem. I'm surprised at myself for being so silly."

The man made no reply but stood, a strong, dark figure, a yard or two from the well, as though waiting for her to join him.

"Come and sit down, sir," cried Olive, patting the brickwork with her small, white hand, "one would think that you did not like your company."

He obeyed slowly and took a seat by her side, drawing so hard at his cigar that the light of it shone upon his fare at every breath. He passed his arm, firm and rigid as steel, behind her, with his hand resting on the brickwork beyond.

"Are you warm enough?" he asked tenderly, as she made a little movement. "Pretty fair," she shivered; "one oughtn't to be cold at this time of the year, but there's a cold, damp air comes up from the well."

As she spoke a faint splash sounded from the depths below, and for the second time that evening, she sprang from the well with a little cry of dismay.

"What is it now?" he asked in a fearful voice. He stood by her side and gazed at the well, as though half expecting to see the cause of her alarm emerge from it.

"Oh, my bracelet," she cried in distress, "my poor mother's bracelet. I've dropped it down the well."

"Your bracelet!" repeated Benson, dully. "Your bracelet? The diamond one?"

"The one that was my mother's," said Olive. "Oh, we can get it back surely. We must have the water drained off."

"Your bracelet!" repeated Benson, stupidly.

"Jem," said the girl in terrified tones, "dear Jem, what is the matter?"

For the man she loved was standing regarding her with horror. The moon which touched it was not responsible for all the whiteness of the distorted face, and she shrank back in fear to the edge of the well. He saw her fear and by a mighty effort regained his composure and took her hand.

"Poor little girl," he murmured, "you frightened me. I was not looking when you cried, and I thought that you were slipping from my arms, down—down—"

His voice broke, and the girl throwing herself into his arms clung to him convulsively.

"There, there," said Benson, fondly, "don't cry, don't cry."

"To-morrow," said Olive, half-laughing, half-crying, "we will all come round the well with hook and line and fish for it. It will be quite a new sport."

"No, we must try some other way," said Benson. "You shall have it back."

"How?" asked the girl.

"You shall see," said Benson. "To-morrow morning at latest you shall have it back. Till then promise me that you will not mention your loss to anyone. Promise."

"I promise," said Olive, wonderingly. "But why not?"

"It is of great value, for one thing, and—But there—there are many reasons. For one thing it is my duty to get it for you."

"Wouldn't you like to jump down for it?" she asked mischievously. "Listen."

She stooped for a stone and dropped it down.

"Fancy being where that is now," she said, peering into the blackness; "fancy going round and round like a mouse in a pail, clutching at the slimy sides, with the water filling your mouth, and looking up to the little patch of sky above."

"You had better come in," said Benson, very quietly. "You are developing a taste for the morbid and horrible."

The girl turned, and taking his arm walked slowly in the direction of the house; Mrs. Benson, who was sitting in the porch, rose to receive them.

"You shouldn't have kept her out so long," she said chidingly. "Where have you been?"

"Sitting on the well," said Olive, smiling, "discussing our future."

"I don't believe that place is healthy," said Mrs. Benson, emphatically. "I really think it might be filled in, Jem."

"All right," said her son, slowly. "Pity it wasn't filled in long ago."

He took the chair vacated by his mother as she entered the house with Olive, and with his hands hanging limply over the sides sat in deep thought. After a time he rose, and going upstairs to a room which was set apart for sporting requisites selected a sea fishing line and some hooks and stole softly downstairs again. He walked swiftly across the park in the direction of the well, turning before he entered the shadow of the trees to look back at the lighted windows of the house. Then having arranged his line he sat on the edge of the well and cautiously lowered it.

He sat with his lips compressed, occasionally looking about him in a startled fashion, as though he half expected to see something peering at him from the belt of trees. Time after time he lowered his line until at length in pulling it up he heard a little metallic tinkle against the side of the well.

He held his breath then, and forgetting his fears drew the line in inch by inch, so as not to lose its precious burden. His pulse beat rapidly, and his eyes were bright. As the line came slowly in he saw the catch hanging to the hook, and with a steady hand drew the last few feet in. Then he saw that instead of the bracelet he had hooked a bunch of keys.

With a faint cry he shook them from the hook into the water below, and stood breathing heavily. Not a sound broke the stillness of the night. He walked up and down a bit and stretched his great muscles; then he came back to the well and resumed his task.

For an hour or more the line was lowered without result. In his eagerness he forgot his fears, and with eyes bent down the well fished slowly and carefully. Twice the hook became entangled in something, and was with difficulty released. It caught a third time, and all his efforts failed' to free it. Then he dropped the line down the well, and with head bent walked toward the house.

He went first to the stables at the rear, and then retiring to his room for some time paced restlessly up and down. Then without removing his clothes he flung himself upon the bed and fell into a troubled sleep.

III.

Long before anybody else was astir he arose and stole softly downstairs. The sunlight was stealing in at every crevice, and flashing in long streaks across the darkened rooms. The dining-room into which he looked struck chill and cheerless in the dark yellow light which came through the lowered blinds. He remembered that it had the same appearance when his father lay dead in the house; now, as then, everything seemed ghastly and unreal; the very chairs standing as their occupants had left them the night before seemed to be indulging in some dark communication of ideas.

Slowly and noiselessly he opened the hall door and passed into the fragrant air beyond. The sun was shining on the drenched grass and trees, and a slowly vanishing white mist rolled like smoke about the grounds. For a moment he stood, breathing deeply the sweet air of the morning, and then walked slowly in the direction of the stables.

The rusty creaking of a pump-handle and a spatter of water upon the red-tiled courtyard showed that somebody else was astir, and a few steps farther he beheld a brawny, sandy-haired man gasping wildly under severe self-infliction at the pump.

"Everything ready, George?" he asked quietly.

"Yes, sir," said the man, straightening up suddenly and touching his forehead. "Bob's just finishing the arrangements inside. It's a lovely morning for a dip. The water in that well must be just icy."

"Be as quick as you can," said Benson, impatiently.

"Very good, sir," said George, burnishing his face harshly with a very small towel which had been hanging over the top of the pump. "Hurry up, Bob."

In answer to his summons a man appeared at the door of the stable with a coil of stout rope over his arm and a large metal candlestick in his hand.

"Just to try the air, sir," said George, following his master's glance, "a well gets rather foul sometimes, but if a candle can live down it, a man can."

His master nodded, and the man, hastily pulling up the neck of his shirt and thrusting his arms into his coat, followed him as he led the way slowly to the well.

"Beg pardon, sir," said George, drawing up to his side, "but you are not looking over and above well this morning. If you'll let me go down I'd enjoy the bath."

"No, no," said Benson, peremptorily.

"You ain't fit to go down, sir," persisted his follower. "I've never seen you look so before. Now if—"

"Mind your business," said his master curtly.

George became silent and the three walked with swinging strides through the long wet grass to the well. Bob flung the rope on the ground and at a sign from his master handed him the candlestick.

"Here's the line for it, sir," said Bob, fumbling in his pockets.

Benson took it from him and slowly tied it to the candlestick. Then he placed it on the edge of the well, and striking a match, lit the candle and began slowly to lower it.

"Hold hard, sir," said George, quickly, laying his hand on his arm, "you must tilt it or the string'll burn through."

Even as he spoke the string parted and the candlestick fell into the water below.

Benson swore quietly.

"I'll soon get another," said George, starting up.

"Never mind, the well's all right," said Benson.

"It won't take a moment, sir," said the other over his shoulder.

"Are you master here, or am I?" said Benson hoarsely.

George came back slowly, a glance at his master's face stopping the protest upon his tongue, and he stood by watching him sulkily as he sat on the well and removed his outer garments. Both men watched him curiously, as having completed his preparations he stood grim and silent with his hands by his sides.

"I wish you'd let me go, sir," said George, plucking up courage to address him. "You ain't fit to go, you've got a chill or something. I shouldn't wonder it's the typhoid. They've got it in the village bad."

For a moment Benson looked at him angrily, then his gaze softened. "Not this time, George," he said, quietly. He took the looped end of the rope and placed it under his arms, and sitting down threw one leg over the side of the well.

"How are you going about it, sir?" queried George, laying hold of the rope and signing to Bob to do the same.

"I'll call out when I reach the water," said Benson; "then pay out three yards more quickly so that I can get to the bottom."

"Very good, sir," answered both.

Their master threw the other leg over the coping and sat motionless. His back was turned toward the men as he sat with head bent, looking down the shaft. He sat for so long that George became uneasy.

"All right sir?" he inquired.

"Yes," said Benson, slowly. "If I tug at the rope, George, pull up at once. Lower away."

The rope passed steadily through their hands until a hollow cry from the darkness below and a faint splashing warned them that he had reached the water. They gave him three yards more and stood with relaxed grasp and strained ears, waiting.

"He's gone under," said Bob in a low voice.

The other nodded, and moistening his huge palms took a firmer grip of the rope.

Fully a minute passed, and the men began to exchange uneasy glances. Then a sudden tremendous jerk followed by a series of feebler ones nearly tore the rope from their grasp.

"Pull!" shouted George, placing one foot on the side and hauling desperately. "Pull! pull! He's stuck fast; he's not coming; PULL!"

In response to their terrific exertions the rope came slowly in, inch by inch, until at length a violent splashing was heard, and at the same moment a scream of unutterable horror came echoing up the shaft.

"What a weight he is !" panted Bob. "He's stuck fast or something. Keep still, sir; for heaven's sake, keep still."

For the taut rope was being jerked violently by the struggles of the weight at the end of it. Both men with grunts and sighs hauled it in foot by foot.

"All right, sir," cried George, cheerfully.

He had one foot against the well, and was pulling manfully; the burden was nearing the top. A long pull and a strong pull, and the face of a dead man with mud in the eyes and nostrils came peering over the edge. Behind it was the ghastly face of his master; but this he saw too late, for with a great cry he let go his hold of the rope and stepped back. The suddenness overthrew his assistant, and the rope tore through his hands. There was a frightful splash.

"You fool!" stammered Bob, and ran to the well helplessly.

"Run!" cried George. "Run for another line."

He bent over the coping and called eagerly down as his assistant sped back to the stables shouting wildly. His voice re-echoed down the shaft, but all else was silence.

THE WHITE CAT

The traveller stood looking from the tap-room window of the *Cauliflower* at the falling rain. The village street below was empty, and everything was quiet with the exception of the garrulous old man smoking with much enjoyment on the settle behind him.

"It'll do a power o' good," said the ancient, craning his neck round the edge of the settle and turning a bleared eye on the window. "I ain't like some folk; I never did mind a drop o' rain."

The traveller grunted and, returning to the settle opposite the old man, fell to lazily stroking a cat which had strolled in attracted by the warmth of the small fire which smouldered in the grate.

"He's a good mouser," said the old man, "but I expect that Smith the landlord would sell 'im to anybody for arf a crown; but we 'ad a cat in Claybury once that you couldn't ha' bought for a hundred golden sovereigns."

The traveller continued to caress the cat.

"A white cat, with one yaller eye and one blue one," continued the old man. "It sounds queer, but it's as true as I sit 'ere wishing that I 'ad another mug o' ale as good as the last you gave me."

The traveller, with a start that upset the cat's nerves, finished his own mug, and then ordered both to be refilled. He stirred the fire into a blaze, and, lighting his pipe and putting one foot on to the hob, prepared to listen.

It used to belong to old man Clark, young Joe Clark's uncle, said the ancient, smacking his lips delicately over the ale and extending a tremulous claw to the tobacco-pouch pushed towards him; and he was never tired of showing it off to people. He used to call it 'is blue-eyed darling, and the fuss 'e made o' that cat was sinful.

Young Joe Clark couldn't bear it, but being down in 'is uncle's will for five cottages and a bit o' land bringing in about forty pounds a year, he 'ad to 'ide his feelings and pretend as he loved it. He used to take it little drops o' cream and tit-bits o' meat, and old Clark was so pleased that 'e promised 'im that he should 'ave the cat along with all the other property when 'e was dead.

Young Joe said he couldn't thank 'im enough, and the old man, who 'ad been ailing a long time, made 'im come up every day to teach 'im 'ow to take care of it arter he was gone. He taught Joe 'ow to cook its meat and then chop it up fine; 'ow it liked a clean saucer every time for its milk; and 'ow he wasn't to make a noise when it was asleep.

"Take care your children don't worry it, Joe," he ses one day, very sharp. "One o' your boys was pulling its tail this morning, and I want you to clump his 'ead for 'im."

"Which one was it?" ses Joe.

"The slobbery-nosed one," ses old Clark.

"I'll give 'im a clout as soon as I get 'ome," ses Joe, who was very fond of 'is children.

"Go and fetch 'im and do it 'ere," ses the old man; "that'll teach 'im to love animals."

Joe went off 'ome to fetch the boy, and arter his mother 'ad washed his face, and wiped his nose, an' put a clean pinneyfore on 'im, he took 'im to 'is uncle's and clouted his 'ead for 'im. Arter that Joe and 'is wife 'ad words all night long, and next morning old Clark, coming in from the garden, was just in time to see 'im kick the cat right acrost the kitchen.

He could 'ardly speak for a minute, and when 'e could Joe see plain wot a fool he'd been. Fust of all 'e called Joe every name he could think of— which took 'im a long time—and then he ordered 'im out of 'is house.

"You shall 'ave my money wen your betters have done with it," he ses, "and not afore. That's all you've done for yourself."

Joe Clark didn't know wot he meant at the time, but when old Clark died three months arterwards 'e found out. His uncle 'ad made a new will and left everything to old George Barstow for as long as the cat lived, providing that he took care of it. When the cat was dead the property was to go to Joe.

The cat was only two years old at the time, and George Barstow, who was arf crazy with joy, said it shouldn't be 'is fault if it didn't live another twenty years.

The funny thing was the quiet way Joe Clark took it. He didn't seem to be at all cut up about it, and when Henery Walker said it was a shame, 'e said he didn't mind, and that George Barstow was a old man, and he was quite welcome to 'ave the property as long as the cat lived.

"It must come to me by the time I'm an old man," he ses, "ard that's all I care about."

Henery Walker went off, and as 'e passed the cottage where old Clark used to live, and which George Barstow 'ad moved into, 'e spoke to the old man over the palings and told 'im wot Joe Clark 'ad said. George Barstow only grunted and went on stooping and prying over 'is front garden.

"Bin and lost something?" ses Henery Walker, watching 'im.

"No; I'm finding," ses George Barstow, very fierce, and picking up something. "That's the fifth bit o' powdered liver I've found in my garden this morning."

Henery Walker went off whistling, and the opinion he'd 'ad o' Joe Clark began to improve. He spoke to Joe about it that arternoon, and Joe said that if 'e ever accused 'im o' such a thing again he'd knock 'is 'ead off. He said that he 'oped the cat 'ud live to be a hundred, and that 'e'd no more think of giving it poisoned meat than Henery Walker would of paying for 'is drink so long as 'e could get anybody else to do it for 'im.

They 'ad bets up at this 'ere *Cauliflower* public-'ouse that evening as to 'ow long that cat 'ud live. Nobody gave it more than a month, and Bill Chambers sat and thought o' so many ways o' killing it on the sly that it was wunnerful to hear 'im.

George Barstow took fright when he 'eard of them, and the care 'e took o' that cat was wunnerful to behold. Arf its time it was shut up in the back bedroom, and the other arf George Barstow was fussing arter it till that cat got to hate 'im like pison. Instead o' giving up work as he'd thought to do, 'e told Henery Walker that 'e'd never worked so 'ard in his life.

"Wot about fresh air and exercise for it?" ses Henery.

"Wot about Joe Clark?" ses George Bar-stow. "I'm tied 'and and foot. I dursent leave the house for a moment. I ain't been to the *Cauliflower* since I've 'ad it, and three times I got out o' bed last night to see if it was safe."

"Mark my words," ses Henery Walker; "if that cat don't 'ave exercise, you'll lose it.

"I shall lose it if it does 'ave exercise," ses George Barstow, "that I know."

He sat down thinking arter Henery Walker 'ad gone, and then he 'ad a little collar and chain made for it, and took it out for a walk. Pretty nearly every dog in Claybury went with 'em, and the cat was in such a state o' mind afore they got 'ome he couldn't do anything with it. It 'ad a fit as soon as they got indoors, and George Barstow, who 'ad read about children's fits in the almanac, gave it a warm bath. It brought it round immediate, and then it began to tear round the room and up and downstairs till George Barstow was afraid to go near it.

It was so bad that evening, sneezing, that George Barstow sent for Bill Chambers, who'd got a good name for doctoring animals, and asked 'im to give it something. Bill said he'd got some powders at 'ome that would cure it at once, and he went and fetched 'em and mixed one up with a bit o' butter.

"That's the way to give a cat medicine," he ses; "smear it with the butter and then it'll lick it off, powder and all."

He was just going to rub it on the cat when George Barstow caught 'old of 'is arm and stopped 'im.

"How do I know it ain't pison?" he ses. "You're a friend o' Joe Clark's, and for all I know he may ha' paid you to pison it."

"I wouldn't do such a thing," ses Bill. "You ought to know me better than that."

"All right," ses George Barstow; "you eat it then, and I'll give you two shillings in stead o' one. You can easy mix some more."

"Not me," ses Bill Chambers, making a face.

"Well, three shillings, then," ses George Barstow, getting more and more suspicious like; "four shillings—five shillings."

Bill Chambers shook his 'ead, and George Barstow, more and more certain that he 'ad caught 'im trying to kill 'is cat and that 'e wouldn't eat the stuff, rose 'im up to ten shillings.

Bill looked at the butter and then 'e looked at the ten shillings on the table, and at last he shut 'is eyes and gulped it down and put the money in 'is pocket.

"You see, I 'ave to be careful, Bill," ses George Barstow, rather upset.

Bill Chambers didn't answer 'im. He sat there as white as a sheet, and making such extraordinary faces that George was arf afraid of 'im.

"Anything wrong, Bill?" he ses at last.

Bill sat staring at 'im, and then all of a sudden he clapped 'is 'andkerchief to 'is mouth and, getting up from his chair, opened the door and rushed out. George Barstow thought at fust that he 'ad eaten pison for the sake o' the ten shillings, but when 'e remembered that Bill Chambers 'ad got the most delikit stummick in Claybury he altered 'is mind.

The cat was better next morning, but George Barstow had 'ad such a fright about it 'e wouldn't let it go out of 'is sight, and Joe Clark began to think that 'e would 'ave to wait longer for that property than 'e had thought, arter all. To 'ear 'im talk anybody'd ha' thought that 'e loved that cat. We didn't pay much attention to it up at the *Cauliflower* 'ere, except maybe to wink at 'im—a thing he couldn't a bear—but at 'ome, o' course, his young 'uns thought as everything he said was Gospel; and one day, coming 'ome from work, as he was passing George Barstow's he was paid out for his deceitfulness.

"I've wronged you, Joe Clark," ses George Barstow, coming to the door, "and I'm sorry for it."

"Oh!" ses Joe, staring.

"Give that to your little Jimmy," ses George Barstow, giving 'im a shilling. "I've give 'im one, but I thought arterwards it wasn't enough."

"What for?" ses Joe, staring at 'im agin.

"For bringing my cat 'ome," ses George Barstow. "'Ow it got out I can't think, but I lost it for three hours, and I'd about given it up when your little Jimmy brought it to me in 'is arms. He's a fine little chap and 'e does you credit."

Joe Clark tried to speak, but he couldn't get a word out, and Henery Walker, wot 'ad just come up and 'eard wot passed, took hold of 'is arm and helped 'im home. He walked like a man in a dream, but arf-way he stopped and cut a stick from the hedge to take 'ome to little Jimmy. He said the boy 'ad been asking him for a stick for some time, but up till then 'e'd always forgotten it.

At the end o' the fust year that cat was still alive, to everybody's surprise; but George Barstow took such care of it 'e never let it out of 'is sight. Every time 'e went out he took it with 'im in a hamper, and, to prevent its being pisoned, he paid Isaac Sawyer, who 'ad the biggest family in Claybury, sixpence a week to let one of 'is boys taste its milk before it had it.

The second year it was ill twice, but the horse-doctor that George Barstow got for it said that it was as 'ard as nails, and with care it might live to be twenty. He said that it wanted more fresh air and exercise; but when he 'eard 'ow George Barstow come by it he said that p'r'aps it would live longer indoors arter all.

At last one day, when George Barstow 'ad been living on the fat o' the land for nearly three years, that cat got out agin. George 'ad raised the front-room winder two or three inches to throw something outside, and, afore he knew wot was 'appening, the cat was out-side and going up the road about twenty miles an hour.

George Barstow went arter it, but he might as well ha' tried to catch the wind. The cat was arf wild with joy at getting out agin, and he couldn't get within arf a mile of it.

He stayed out all day without food or drink, follering it about until it came on dark, and then, o' course, he lost sight of it, and, hoping against 'ope that it would come home for its food, he went 'ome and waited for it. He sat up all night dozing in a chair in the front room with the door left open, but it was all no use; and arter thinking for a long time wot was best to do, he went out and told some o' the folks it was lost and offered a reward of five pounds for it.

You never saw such a hunt then in all your life. Nearly every man, woman, and child in Claybury left their work or school and went to try and earn that five pounds. By the arternoon George Barstow made it ten pounds provided the cat was brought 'ome safe and sound, and people as was too old to walk stood at their cottage doors to snap it up as it came by.

Joe Clark was hunting for it 'igh and low, and so was 'is wife and the boys. In fact, I b'lieve that everybody in Claybury excepting the parson and Bob Pretty was trying to get that ten pounds.

O' course, we could understand the parson—'is pride wouldn't let 'im; but a low, poaching, thieving rascal like Bob Pretty turning up 'is nose at ten pounds was more than we could make out. Even on the second day, when George Barstow made it ten pounds down and a shilling a week for a year besides, he didn't offer to stir; all he did was to try and make fun o' them as was looking for it.

"Have you looked everywhere you can think of for it, Bill?" he ses to Bill Chambers. "Yes, I 'ave," ses Bill.

"Well, then, you want to look everywhere else," ses Bob Pretty. "I know where I should look if I wanted to find it."

"Why don't you find it, then?" ses Bill.

"'Cos I don't want to make mischief," ses Bob Pretty. "I don't want to be unneighbourly to Joe Clark by interfering at all."

"Not for all that money?" ses Bill.

"Not for fifty pounds," ses Bob Pretty; "you ought to know me better than that, Bill Chambers."

"It's my belief that you know more about where that cat is than you ought to," ses Joe Gubbins.

"You go on looking for it, Joe," ses Bob Pretty, grinning; "it's good exercise for you, and you've only lost two days' work."

"I'll give you arf a crown if you let me search your 'ouse, Bob," ses Bill Chambers, looking at 'im very 'ard.

"I couldn't do it at the price, Bill," ses Bob Pretty, shaking his 'ead. "I'm a pore man, but I'm very partikler who I 'ave come into my 'ouse."

O' course, everybody left off looking at once when they heard about Bob— not that they believed that he'd be such a fool as to keep the cat in his 'ouse; and that evening, as soon as it was dark, Joe Clark went round to see 'im.

"Don't tell me as that cat's found, Joe," ses Bob Pretty, as Joe opened the door.

"Not as I've 'eard of," said Joe, stepping inside. "I wanted to speak to you about it; the sooner it's found the better I shall be pleased."

"It does you credit, Joe Clark," ses Bob Pretty.

"It's my belief that it's dead," ses Joe, looking at 'im very 'ard; "but I want to make sure afore taking over the property."

Bob Pretty looked at 'im and then he gave a little cough. "Oh, you want it to be found dead," he ses. "Now, I wonder whether that cat's worth most dead or alive?"

Joe Clark coughed then. "Dead, I should think," he ses at last. "George Barstow's just 'ad bills printed offering fifteen pounds for it," ses Bob Pretty.

"I'll give that or more when I come into the property," ses Joe Clark.

"There's nothing like ready-money, though, is there?" ses Bob.

"I'll promise it to you in writing, Bob," ses Joe, trembling.

"There's some things that don't look well in writing, Joe," says Bob Pretty, considering; "besides, why should you promise it to me?"

"O' course, I meant if you found it," ses Joe.

"Well, I'll do my best, Joe," ses Bob Pretty; "and none of us can do no more than that, can they?"

They sat talking and argufying over it for over an hour, and twice Bob Pretty got up and said 'e was going to see whether George Barstow wouldn't offer more. By the time they parted they was as thick as thieves, and next morning Bob Pretty was wearing Joe Clark's watch and chain, and Mrs. Pretty was up at Joe's 'ouse to see whether there was any of 'is furniture as she 'ad a fancy for.

She didn't seem to be able to make up 'er mind at fust between a chest o' drawers that 'ad belonged to Joe's mother and a grand-father clock. She walked from one to the other for about ten minutes, and then Bob, who 'ad come in to 'elp her, told 'er to 'ave both.

"You're quite welcome," he ses; "ain't she, Joe?"

Joe Clark said "Yes," and arter he 'ad helped them carry 'em 'ome the Prettys went back and took the best bedstead to pieces, cos Bob said as it was easier to carry that way. Mrs. Clark 'ad to go and sit down at the bottom o' the garden with the neck of 'er dress undone to give herself air, but when she saw the little Prettys each walking 'ome with one of 'er best chairs on their 'eads she got and walked up and down like a mad thing.

"I'm sure I don't know where we are to put it all," ses Bob Pretty to Joe Gubbins, wot was looking on with other folks, "but Joe Clark is that generous he won't 'ear of our leaving anything."

"Has 'e gorn mad?" ses Bill Chambers, staring at 'im.

"Not as I knows on," ses Bob Pretty. "It's 'is good-'artedness, that's all. He feels sure that that cat's dead, and that he'll 'ave George Barstow's cottage and furniture. I told 'im he'd better wait till he'd made sure, but 'e wouldn't."

Before they'd finished the Prettys 'ad picked that 'ouse as clean as a bone, and Joe Clark 'ad to go and get clean straw for his wife and children to sleep on; not that Mrs. Clark 'ad any sleep that night, nor Joe neither.

Henery Walker was the fust to see what it really meant, and he went rushing off as fast as 'e could run to tell George Barstow. George couldn't believe 'im at fust, but when 'e did he swore that if a 'air of that cat's head was harmed 'e'd 'ave the law o' Bob Pretty, and arter Henery Walker 'ad gone 'e walked round to tell 'im so.

"You're not yourself, George Barstow, else you wouldn't try and take away my character like that," ses Bob Pretty.

"Wot did Joe Clark give you all them things for?" ses George, pointing to the furniture.

"Took a fancy to me, I s'pose," ses Bob. "People do sometimes. There's something about me at times that makes 'em like me."

"He gave 'em to you to kill my cat," ses George Barstow. "It's plain enough for any-body to see."

Bob Pretty smiled. "I expect it'll turn up safe and sound one o' these days," he ses, "and then you'll come round and beg my pardon. P'r'aps—"

"P'r'aps wot?" ses George Barstow, arter waiting a bit.

"P'r'aps somebody 'as got it and is keeping it till you've drawed the fifteen pounds out o' the bank," ses Bob, looking at 'im very hard.

"I've taken it out o' the bank," ses George, starting; "if that cat's alive, Bob, and you've got it, there's the fifteen pounds the moment you 'and it over."

"Wot d'ye mean—me got it?" ses Bob Pretty. "You be careful o' my character."

"I mean if you know where it is," ses George Barstow trembling all over.

"I don't say I couldn't find it, if that's wot you mean," ses Bob. "I can gin'rally find things when I want to."

"You find me that cat, alive and well, and the money's yours, Bob," ses George, 'ardly able to speak, now that 'e fancied the cat was still alive.

Bob Pretty shook his 'ead. "No; that won't do," he ses. "S'pose I did 'ave the luck to find that pore animal, you'd say I'd had it all the time and refuse to pay."

"I swear I wouldn't, Bob," ses George Barstow, jumping up.

"Best thing you can do if you want me to try and find that cat," says Bob Pretty, "is to give me the fifteen pounds now, and I'll go and look for it at once. I can't trust you, George Barstow."

"And I can't trust you," ses George Barstow.

"Very good," ses Bob, getting up; "there's no 'arm done. P'r'aps Joe Clark 'll find the cat is dead and p'r'aps you'll find it's alive. It's all one to me."

George Barstow walked off 'ome, but he was in such a state o' mind 'e didn't know wot to do. Bob Pretty turning up 'is nose at fifteen pounds like that made 'im think that Joe Clark 'ad promised to pay 'im more if the cat was dead; and at last, arter worrying about it for a couple o' hours, 'e came up to this 'ere *Cauliflower* and offered Bob the fifteen pounds.

"Wot's this for?" ses Bob.

"For finding my cat," ses George.

"Look here," ses Bob, handing it back, "I've 'ad enough o' your insults; I don't know where your cat is."

"I mean for trying to find it, Bob," ses George Barstow.

"Oh, well, I don't mind that," ses Bob, taking it. "I'm a 'ard-working man, and I've got to be paid for my time; it's on'y fair to my wife and children. I'll start now."

He finished up 'is beer, and while the other chaps was telling George Barstow wot a fool he was Joe Clark slipped out arter Bob Pretty and began to call 'im all the names he could think of.

"Don't you worry," ses Bob; "the cat ain't found yet."

"Is it dead?" ses Joe Clark, 'ardly able to speak.

"'Ow should I know?" ses Bob; "that's wot I've got to try and find out. That's wot you gave me your furniture for, and wot George Barstow gave me the fifteen pounds for, ain't it? Now, don't you stop me now, 'cos I'm goin' to begin looking."

He started looking there and then, and for the next two or three days George Barstow and Joe Clark see 'im walking up and down with his 'ands in 'is pockets looking over garden fences and calling "Puss." He asked everybody 'e see whether they 'ad seen a white cat with one blue eye and one yaller one, and every time 'e came into the *Cauliflower* he put his 'ead over the bar and called "Puss," 'cos, as 'e said, it was as likely to be there as anywhere else.

It was about a week after the cat 'ad disappeared that George Barstow was standing at 'is door talking to Joe Clark, who was saying the cat must be dead and 'e wanted 'is property, when he sees a man coming up the road carrying a basket stop and speak to Bill Chambers. Just as 'e got near them an awful "miaow" come from the basket and George Barstow and Joe Clark started as if they'd been shot.

"He's found it?" shouts Bill Chambers, pointing to the man.

"It's been living with me over at Ling for a week pretty nearly," ses the man. "I tried to drive it away several times, not knowing that there was fifteen pounds offered for it."

George Barstow tried to take 'old of the basket.

"I want that fifteen pounds fust," ses the man.

"That's on'y right and fair, George," ses Bob Pretty, who 'ad just come up. "You've got all the luck, mate. We've been hunting 'igh and low for that cat for a week."

Then George Barstow tried to explain to the man and call Bob Pretty names at the same time; but it was all no good. The man said it 'ad nothing to do with 'im wot he 'ad paid to Bob Pretty; and at last they fetched Policeman White over from Cudford, and George Barstow signed a paper to pay five shillings a week till the reward was paid.

George Barstow 'ad the cat for five years arter that, but he never let it get away agin. They got to like each other in time and died within a fortnight of each other, so that Joe Clark got 'is property arter all.

W.W. Jacobs – A Short Biography

William Wymark Jacobs was born on September 8, 1863 in the Wapping district of London, England. An author, humorist and dramatist, Jacobs is best remembered for the enduring classic tale of horror - "The Monkey's Paw".

As a youth, Jacobs grew up near the Wapping docks in London, where his father was a wharf manager. The family's first home was home was a house on a River Thames wharf.

The docklands setting would show up frequently in his later literary output. Jacobs, the wharf rat, and his three siblings lost their mother when they were all still young children. Their father, William Gage Jacobs, remarried and fathered a further seven children with his erstwhile housekeeper Ellen Florey. Although he grew up surrounded by poverty, Jacobs himself received a formal education in London, first at a private prep school and later at the Birkbeck Literary and Scientific Institute (now part of the University of London and known as Birkbeck College).

Jacobs' adult working life began with a clerical position at the Post Office Savings Bank. The job was not a stimulating one but Jacobs put his imagination to good use and started to write short stories, sketches and articles, many of which appeared in the Post Office house publication "Blackfriars Magazine."

Although Jacobs did receive his fair share of rejection slips at the beginning of his career, many works written during this period of clerical employment appeared in the "Idler" and "Today" magazines, both of which were edited by noted humorist Jerome K. Jerome, who had taken a liking to Jacobs' stories.

From 1898, Jacobs also published stories in "The Strand", a popular, monthly fiction and general interest magazine. The arrangement stayed in place for most of his life and many of the works in Jacobs' subsequent collections – including the nautical serialization A Master of Craft (1899-1900) - appeared there first.

Jacobs' first volume of collected works was published in 1896. Many Cargoes, a selection of sea-faring yarns, established Jacobs as a popular writer and humorist with a penchant for authentic dialogue and trick endings (critics of the day referred to him as the "O. Henry of the Waterfront").

A year later he published a novelette, The Skipper's Wooing, and in 1898 and another collection of short stories titled Sea Urchins. These works painted vivid, if imaginatively stretched, pictures of dockland and seafaring London with colourful characters (such as "The Night Watchman", Ginger Dick) that now seem archetypal.

Many of Jacobs' periodical publications and first editions were illustrated with woodcuts and ink drawings, as was still the custom at the turn of the 20th century. The author worked regularly with artists such as E.W. Kemble, who had illustrated Mark Twain's Adventures of Huckleberry Finn and Harriet Beecher Stowe's Uncle Tom's Cabin, and his good friend Will Owen, who eventually became a household name on the strength of his iconic Bisto Kids, Bovril and Lux Soap advertising posters.

By 1899, Jacobs was able to quit the post office and finally begin a career making a living as a full-time writer.

He married the noted suffragist Agnes Eleanor Williams (who had been jailed for her protest activities) in 1900. They set up a household in Loughton, Essex as well as living part of the year in central London. The couple went on to have five children together though their marriage was considered an unhappy one.

The publication of two short novels: At Sunwich Port (a romantic tale of rival sea captains in the fictional seaside community of Sunwich standing in for the actual East England community of Sandwich, Kent) and Dialstone Lane (another small town romance involving intrigue and buried treasure), in 1902 and 1904 respectively, cemented Jacobs' reputation as one of the leading British authors of the new century.

On the foundations of a continuing ability to write for his audience he was readily published though he never strayed too far from what was becoming his familiar, dependable style. There followed a string of further successful publications, including Captain's All (1905), Night Watches (1914), The Castaways (1916), and Sea Whispers (1926). Jacobs published eighteen books in all during his lifetime; thirteen collections and five novels.

As a storyteller, Jacobs is perhaps better remembered for a handful of brief tales of the supernatural than for his popular nautical-themed works. The most famous of these, The Monkey's Paw, originally appeared as part of the 1902 short story collection The Lady of the Barge. It is an economically written story about a shriveled talisman, a monkey's paw that brings grief and horror in the wake of all too literal wish granting. The story has been adapted for other media repeatedly, starting with a one-act play performed at London's Haymarket Theatre in 1903. There have been multiple film adaptations of the story in the modern era; some of us are familiar with its appearance in an episode of the popular animated series, The Simpsons.

Another macabre gem, The Toll-House, was published as part of the collection Sailor's Knots in 1909. Jacob's once again employs a sparse style to tell the story of a group of men who spend the night in a famously haunted house on a dare (a noticeably similar narrative concept was put to use in the much earlier play The Ghost of Jerry Bundler, which had launched Jacobs' parallel career as a dramatist back in 1899 when it was produced at the St. James Theatre in London). Innovative at the time of writing, these sparingly written, atmospheric ghost stories are now familiar classics of the supernatural genre.

Though prolific in his younger years, Jacobs' productivity dropped dramatically after the start of World War I. Yet even in self-imposed semi-retirement Jacobs was still recognized as a leading humorist, ranked alongside such writers as P. G. Wodehouse and George Birmingham. He enjoyed continuing influence and elevated status among his fellow writers as evidenced by these comments attributed to his colleague Henry James:

"Mr. Jacobs, I envy you. You are popular! Your admirable work is appreciated by a wide circle of readers; it has achieved popularity. Mine never goes into a second edition."

James' literary fortunes would, of course, change, but his back-handedly complimentary admiration is compelling evidence of Jacobs' reputation as a writer and humourist both for his audience and his perhaps more admired literary colleagues.

Though Jacobs would create little in the way of new work after 1911, he was still writing. In these later years, seemingly burnt out creatively, Jacobs concentrated more on writing dramatizations and adaptations of his existing stories, including Beauty and the Barge (a film version starring Margaret Rutherford was also released in 1937) and In the Dark (a one act play that is often performed pr published with The Monkey's Paw adaptation).

Though admired by loyal readers throughout his lifetime, Jacobs has been almost completely forgotten since. Critics are at a loss to name a single reason why - Jacobs is universally considered to be a fine and imaginative literary craftsman. But, as critic John Wain suggested in a 1960 essay, perhaps Jacobs' humour may have been too gentle to persist into the cruel and sarcastic modern era, his dry pokes at proletariat hardship no longer suiting the times.

Nonetheless, Jacobs' legacy remains solid: he continued Dickens' (a writer with whom he is also often compared) tradition for sharing working class stories in authentic vernacular. And polished narratives such as The Monkey's Paw set a standard for the clever use of horror in fiction and popular culture that endures to this day. Indeed recently his works have begun to show an increased demand and appreciation in a world that is constantly looking over its shoulder.

William Wymark Jacobs died in a North London nursing home in Hornsey Lane, Islington on September 1st, 1943, just a week before his 80th birthday.

W.W. Jacobs – A Concise Bibliography

NOVELS AND SHORT STORY COLLECTIONS
MANY CARGOES (SHORT STORIES) (1896)
THE SKIPPER'S WOOING (1897)
SEA URCHINS (SHORT STORIES) (1898) aka MORE CARGOES
A MASTER OF CRAFT (1900)
LIGHT FREIGHTS (SHORT STORIES) (1901)
THE LADY OF THE BARGE (SHORT STORIES) (1902)
AT SUNWICH PORT (1902)
DIALSTONE LANE (1902)
SALTHAVEN (1908)
CAPTAINS ALL (SHORT STORIES) (1911)
NIGHT WATCHERS (SHORT STORIES) (1914)
DEEP WATERS (SHORT STORIES) (1919)

SHORT STORIES (INCLUDING THOSE USED IN THE COLLECTIONS ABOVE)
A BENEFIT PERFORMANCE
A BLACK AFFAIR
A CASE OF DESERTION
A CHANGE OF TREATMENT
A CIRCULAR TOUR
A DISCIPLINARIAN
A DISTANT RELATIVE
A GARDEN PLOT
A GOLDEN VENTURE
A HARBOUR OF REFUGE

A LOVE KNOT
A LOVE PASSAGE
A MARKED MAN
A MIXED PROPOSAL
A RASH EXPERIMENT
A SAFETY MATCH
A SPIRIT OF AVARICE
A TIGER'S SKIN
ADMIRAL PETERS
AFTER THE INQUEST
ALF'S DREAM
AN ADULTERATION ACT
AN ELABORATE ELOPEMENT
AN INTERVENTION
AN ODD FREAK
ANGELS' VISITS
BACK TO BACK
BEDRIDDEN
THE WINTER OFFENSIVE
THE BEQUEST
BILL'S LAPSE
BILL'S PAPER CHASE
BLUNDELL'S IMPROVEMENT
THE BOATSWAIN'S WATCH
THE BOATSWAIN'S MATE
BOB'S REDEMPTION
BREAKING A SPELL
BREVET RANK
BROTHER HUTCHINS
THE BULLY OF THE "CAVENDISH"
THE CABIN PASSENGER
CAPTAIN ROGERS
THE CAPTAIN'S EXPLOIT
CAPTAINS ALL
THE CASTAWAY
THE CHANGELING
"CHOICE SPIRITS"
THE CONSTABLE'S MOVE
CONTRABAND OF WAR
THE CONVERT
THE COOK OF THE "GANNET"
CUPBOARD LOVE
DESERTED
DIRTY WORK
THE DISBURSEMENT SHEET
DIXON'S RETURN
DOUBLE DEALING
THE DREAMER
DUAL CONTROL
EASY MONEY
ESTABLISHING RELATIONS

RULE OF THREE
SAM'S BOY
SAM'S GHOST
SELF-HELP
SENTENCE DEFERRED
SHAREHOLDERS
SKILLED ASSISTANCE
THE SKIPPER OF THE "OSPREY"
SMOKED SKIPPER
STEPPING BACKWARDS
STRIKING HARD
THE SUBSTITUTE
THE TEMPTATION OF SAMUEL BURGE
THE TEST
THE THREE SISTERS
TO HAVE AND TO HOLD
"THE TOLL-HOUSE"
TWIN SPIRITS
TWO OF A TRADE
THE UNDERSTUDY
THE UNKNOWN
THE VIGIL
WATCH-DOGS
THE WEAKER VESSEL
THE WELL
THE WHITE CAT

STAGE
THE GHOST OF JERRY BUNDLER (1899) (In London)

FILM ADAPTATIONS
A MASTER OF CRAFT (1922)
THE MONKEY'S PAW (1933)
OUR RELATIONS, a Laurel & Hardy film, "suggested by" to Jacobs' "The Money Box." (1936)
FOOTSTEPS IN THE FOG, from the short story The Interruption. (1955)

www.ingramcontent.com/pod-product-compliance
Lightning Source LLC
Chambersburg PA
CBHW071326130626
46556CB00004B/1770